MISTLETOE MISMATCH

MISTLETOE MISMATCH

A MISTLETOE KISSES ROMANCE

E.B. SILVA

THE MISTLETOE KISSES SERIES

Check Out The Remaining Books in The Mistletoe Kisses Series

The "Mistletoe Kisses" series, a collection of 38 heartwarming clean romance stories that will make your spirits bright. Featuring popular tropes such as Fake Dating, friends to lovers, grumpy sunshine, accidental marriages, cowboys, Christmas magic, and so so much more!

Fate brings together couples who discover the true meaning of Christmas, but first, they must navigate the festive season and their own hesitations. As they find themselves under the mistletoe, they learn that sometimes, all it takes is one kiss to change everything.

"Mistletoe Kisses" - Where one kiss can change everything.

CHECK OUT THE REST OF THE SERIES HERE

CHAPTER
ONE
CHASE

"It's not half bad," Eldon grunts, standing over my shoulder. His form casts an unwelcome shadow on the page, bringing my graphite-blackened fingers to a halt and a frown to my face.

The midday sun blares down on us, white and ethereal —in no way easing the bone-numbing cold of a late December morning in southwestern Colorado.

Bringing my hands close to my mouth, I blow precious heat into my frozen fingertips, grumbling, "Thankfully, you're better at cow punching than judging art."

His rough, work-hardened hand grazes over his chin, the calluses on his palm and fingertips scratching against his gray and white afternoon stubble.

I look up, catching the old man's silver eyes, fast as mercury, and he shrugs. The lines cut deep in his windswept brow. "Better than I could do," he growls.

I chuckle. "You've got me there, old man."

Eldon's as much a facet of Heart's Desire Ranch as the towering snow-dusted, red-washed San Juan Mountains,

1

encircling the sprawling city of Ouray nestled in the valley below.

Gold Mountain cradles the ranch four generations of ancestors built with blood, sweat, and grit. The location affords sweeping three hundred and sixty-degree views. Expansive views, chest swelling views that remind me with every breath of the bracing air what the Hearts have sacrificed to keep and hold this spot.

Poised above seven thousand feet, I can't sit still for long. Either I'm in the saddle or pawing through my notebook for a free page to sketch the distant peaks—like spectacular, scarlet-skinned sirens—or to jot down my more poetic thoughts.

"I still don't understand why people call this neck of the woods the 'Switzerland of America,' do you, Eldon?"

The old man shakes his head. "I suppose I don't have a strong opinion on the matter."

We've had this conversation more times than I can count, but it never gets old. "It boggles the mind to compare this savage beauty with a civilized, tamed locale in Central Europe."

He shakes his head, running his hand over his handlebar mustache.

"No doubt the folks at the tourism board thought up that silly title. But it neglects nature's lattice-work layers of shale, limestone, and sandstone, punctuated by towering evergreens and wind-bent, leafless aspens—"

"Don't go getting all poetical on me, Chase. Piling one big word on top of another the way nature does sediment until I can't make head nor tail of what we're talking about."

"Blame the university for that." I have a Master's in geology, and I wanted to become a science writer. But as the only Heart offspring, I had to take over the family business. "Some locations transform people into poets. I imagine Switzerland is one of them. But this place forges them into geologists, trying with all their might to describe the incomprehensible...*the sublime*..."

"Or figure out where all the gold and silver lie," Eldon adds, alluding to the honeycomb of mines beneath Ouray's surface.

I imagine Ole Chief Ouray, leader of the Tabeguache and Uncompahgre bands of the Utes and namesake of this slice of heaven, would agree with me about the Switzerland comparison. Or he'd call me a fool for letting my mind wander too far. A condition I haven't tamed in forty-plus years of lukewarm trying.

Of course, maybe I'm wrong about all of these reflections. After all, I've never technically been to Switzerland... Neither has Eldon.

With a furtive glance at the black and gray sketch that will never do this hollowed-out, glacial valley justice, I tuck my field notebook away, stretching and rising to my full height. At six foot three, I tower over Eldon. Yet, it doesn't seem that long ago I looked up to this man, both physically and mentally—the strongest, toughest cowboy in the crew.

I rub the spot on my Carhartt directly over my heart. Life is an endless parade of change...the moment you get comfortable or become attached, fate steps in with stomach-churning enthusiasm to wrestle it from you. Like when God stole my wife, Lisa, three winters ago, burning our shared future to the ground and making me a single dad in one fell swoop.

"You've got a distant look in your eyes, Chase. Don't let those thoughts carry you too deep," the old ranch hand warns, heading towards the horses.

He knows better than anyone where my mind mustn't go, having walked with me every step of the way through the slow journey towards my wife's death. A death summed up by the two most sinister and cruel syllables in the English language: cancer.

"Better get back to work before the next storm hits..." My eyes scan the threatening dark band of clouds hammering the distant ridgeline.

Eldon's bushy eyebrows shoot up. "What about a Christmas tree for Maddie?"

I curse under my breath, looking to the side. Fetching our annual Christmas tree used to be something Lisa and I relished every year. Now, it feels like an untenable burden.

"It's for Maddie, Buster."

A flash of anger runs the length of my body, and I bite my tongue hard, fighting the urge to snap at him for using my childhood nickname. I'm master enough of my feelings to know Eldon isn't the source of my current fury. Fate is, fickle and cruel.

After a long pause, the old man asks, "What about that writer lady the tourism board keeps trying to connect you with before Christmas? I could give her a quick tour. Wouldn't take more than an hour or so."

I glare at him, feeling my heart race. Chanel Love, a writer of romance novels and quite possibly the most beautiful woman I've seen in a long while. After the third call from the tourism board, I looked up her website and books. Instant lightning rippled through my computer screen at the sight of her photos, stealing my breath and stopping my heart.

Any other man would fall all over himself to meet her, but that's the last thing on my mind. Because love precedes loss, and the more you love, the more painful the loss. I can't go through it a second time, even though Lisa made me promise to move on after her passing. Despite telling her what she needed to hear, the truth is I only had one great love in me. Living past her means inhabiting a pale, unsatisfying shadow world. Lisa may have left me, but I'm the dead one.

"So, you're just going to ignore her and the tourism board?"

I nod, setting my mouth firmly. Even worse than ignoring her, I've actively worked at avoiding her. When the first gallery owner in town called to let me know the pretty, sunshiny blonde asked about me, I told him to say I'm a "grumpy, old cowboy" and to pass the word along.

While not accurate physically, it is spiritually and emotionally, so I don't feel especially guilty about the half-truth. She should be leaving Ouray any day now. Then, I can quit worrying about bumping into the woman too beautiful to meet.

I take a different tack with Eldon, though. "The last thing this ranch needs is the wrong kind of publicity. Do you want to turn Heart's Desire into Chief Joseph Ranch?" Located in Darby, Montana, they film *Yellowstone* there, with guards lining the gates during filming and tourists flocking to cabins named after the show's main characters in the off-season. *No, thank you!*

The old man counters, "Publicity's publicity. Heart's Desire Foundation could use it."

Eldon refers to the organization I started after my wife's death to ease the financial burdens faced by cancer patients, especially children and their families. I sell my art —originals and prints—in town at local galleries to raise money for the foundation. I also have a self-illustrated book of poetry that brings in decent revenue. Fundraising events throughout the year help us achieve our annual goals while letting me stay out of the limelight. It's a perfect setup for a recluse like me.

Clearing my throat, I ignore Eldon's last statement the same way I've been ignoring the tourism board and Chanel Love. "These fences need mending..."

The ranch foreman nods, his face rigid and his lips pressed tightly together beneath his showy handlebar mustache.

CHAPTER
TWO
CHANEL

The clink of plates, the low rumble of conversation, and the delectable odor of freshly ground and brewing coffee energize me as much as the lavender latte poised on the cafe table before me. The tourist pamphlets couldn't have been more right. Ouray, Colorado, really is the "Switzerland of America." Soon, it will be the setting of my next bestselling cowboy romance series. I feel it in my gut, and my gut's never wrong...

Which makes the current situation even more confounding. Seeking permission from Chase Heart, the owner of Heart's Desire Ranch, to tour his property. I only need a couple of hours to get the inspiration flowing. Most ranchers would jump at the chance of a bestselling author fixating on their location for a potential series. *Hello, merch and tourism!*

Folks from Telluride to Silverton have already offered to stand in, thanks to my personal assistant's persistent calls to locals to facilitate a meeting with Mr. Heart. I can't settle for anything less than his ranch, though. My intuition is never wrong about writing; I'm not about to second-guess myself now.

My eyes focus on Allie, seated across from me. The cute forty-something redhead owns Art Dogs Cafe, an eclectic art studio that serves morning pastries and specialty coffee drinks. She's got an adorable pixie cut I could never pull off and large, cerulean eyes that round when I hold up my most prized literary possession, *Sublime Incantations*. "I see you sell Chase Heart's book here. Does he ever come in? Any chance you could introduce me to him?"

Her tongue darts out to lick her lips, and the rate of her eye blinking doubles. "That grumpy, old cowboy? Why would you want to meet him?"

I sigh, frowning.

Then, she laughs a little, knowing laugh like the joke's on me. Every person in this town has done the same thing, from gallery owners to booksellers to other cafe owners, when I mention the man's name. But nobody's letting me in on what's so funny.

I shake my head, setting his book in my lap. "I'm a fellow writer, and his work speaks to me in ways I can't describe. Beautiful, stunning ways. I want to make his ranch the setting of my next book series. But he's impossible to get a hold of."

She laughs, shaking her head. "Not at all. He came in here yesterday." My heart races at the thought of the cowboy with the brown duster and white hat suddenly walking through the door. That's the only photo I found of him online, with his back toward the camera. Hardly a revealing shot of my enigma. She asks, "What kinds of books do you write?"

"Romances. My pen name is Chanel Love."

"Chanel Love?" Her eyebrows shoot up into her hairline.

"*The* Chanel Love? Oh my goodness! Your books are amazing!"

"Thank you." I try to act happy, but disappointment grips me. I'm at the end of a week-long stay in Ouray. Book signings here and in Telluride, Durango, and Silverton gave me an official reason for the trip. In all actuality, though, I wanted to meet Mr. Heart, get him to sign my book, and tour his ranch. None of these things have happened.

My eyes wander to the photos of his ranch fanned out on the table, sitting on thousands of acres, thousands of feet above sea level. The property includes historic mining claims and rich pastoral land that has nurtured cattle for more than a century.

Allie inquires, "How did you first hear about Chase and Heart's Desire anyway?"

"My cousin Courtney and her boyfriend, Troy, spent the summer backpacking around Ouray County. They stumbled across Heart's Desire Ranch during their trip, snagging these pictures from a distance." I motion towards the images in front of me. "Once I saw them, I was sold."

Courtney also gifted me the book and some prints, introducing me to the infuriatingly beautiful mystery of Chase Heart. His words wrapped around me like a hug, making me believe in crazy, wild, reckless love again— something personal experiences had all but squashed. And his artwork made me yearn for sinewy, snow-dusted, scarlet mountain ranges kissing Colorado skies. He felt like a kindred spirit, somebody I needed to meet and spend time with, even if only for a few rounds of Bingo at the retirement home.

Allie's voice pulls me back. "Aren't the photos enough to go by? Why do you need to tour the ranch?"

At the risk of sounding too woo-woo, I reply, "I'm an

energy person. I need to feel what it's like to be there. To stare at the same incredible panoramas Mr. Heart describes in his poems and artwork...to breathe the same air."

She shrugs. "Don't get me wrong. It's a nice place and all. But there are way fancier properties around here, believe me."

"So, you've been there?"

"Of course, I used to...uh...know the family well. Would you like to buy a few more copies of his book to take back home with you? You know, Mr. Heart's foundation does incredible work for cancer patients, with all the proceeds from his book and art sales going to the cause."

"I'll take all five," I reply with my best smile, trying to remain upbeat.

Her eyebrows arch. Maybe I can buy my way into meeting the guy, although time's running out...

I continue, "The foundation sounds amazing. His book is amazing. So is his artwork. I'm just a little frustrated because you'd think having the publicity associated with one of my series set on his ranch would be welcome." The ear-to-ear grin pinned on my face makes my cheeks tremble as exasperation sizzles inside.

Stay cheerful, Chanel. I'm a huge proponent of positivity, but some days take more energy than others.

She chuckles. "It's a Chase thing. Don't take it personally." That's another refrain I've heard a lot of this week.

The bell to the cafe door jingles, and our eyes race to the entrance. A diminutive woman with long brown hair and a school-aged boy and girl stride toward the counter to scrutinize the drink menu on the wall behind the cash register. Allie excuses herself to take their orders.

The coffee table book feels heavy in my lap, as heavy as the sigh that parts my lips. I run my hand over the cover, tracing the wild swirl of one of his geologic drawings. The way he expresses himself on the page, visually and through words, unceasingly captures my soul, no matter how disagreeable the real man may be.

My personal assistant, Sylvia, says I'm stalking him, that I've fallen in obsession and quite possibly love with him. It's a ridiculous thought. The depth of his words and thoughts and the prolific nature of his drawings have me guessing he's at least in his seventies. So do the constant onslaught of "grumpy, old cowboy" comments.

I shake my head, chewing on my pen cap. It's a gross habit but still better than smoking, drinking, or binge eating... Although not according to my ex-boyfriend, Olivier, who cited my uncouthness as one of the reasons for our breakup. The words still ring in my head. *Your manners, Chanel, where are they?*

My favorite part of him leaving, however, remains, and I quote: *I can't imagine spending the rest of my life with a woman who doesn't know the difference between earthy and woodsy tones in her varietals...* Did I mention he was a wine snob?

Chanel and Olivier. It should have gone together like some scrumptious mid-nineties French fragrance commercial. Instead, it crashed and burned, leaving me tired, jaded, and empty.

Relief flooded me in waves during our breakup. Despite ending a five-year relationship, I felt no urge to cry, scream, or binge-watch regency romances with a tub of Ben & Jerry's ice cream. Really, I didn't feel much of anything.

Maybe the consensus of men I've dated over the years is right. I really am an ice princess...*frigid to the core.* It would explain why, at thirty-two, I remain unmarried and childless. In my defense, no guy's ever bowled me over or made me fall so hard I can't think straight.

Ironic, considering I make my living peddling the true love fantasy. It's not that I don't want to believe in it. I do with every part of my being, but I have yet to find evidence for its existence.

Maybe that's why I glommed onto *Sublime Incantations* with such enthusiasm. It made me feel things I hadn't in years, and it made me believe in big, beautiful, all-encompassing love again.

Maybe I need to do lunch at the Ouray Senior Center? Give finding Chase Heart one more shot.

My phone reads eight thirty-five. Not too early to bother my personal assistant, Sylvia. *The definition of insanity is doing the same thing repeatedly while expecting a different outcome.* I text:

> Any luck getting a tour of Heart's Desire?

I wait impatiently as three dots light up the screen, indicating she's typing.

> Here's the final word from the Ouray Tourism Board. It's a working ranch, not a dude ranch, and the owner doesn't want visitors. Sorry

> This guy... I swear. Does he know I'm leaving tomorrow?

> He's probably counting the hours... You've been kinda stalking him after all

> I just need an hour to get a feel for the place

> Yep

And?

> Oh my gosh, Chanel, you can be so difficult sometimes. There are 100 other ranches in the area, with owners ready to roll out the red carpet

Sighing heavily, I scan the photos again. I've wrestled with intuitive revelations my whole life. I can't explain why, but I refuse to settle for less or different...*even if it makes me seem like a diva.*

> Offer money. Do whatever you need to sweeten the deal. I won't bother a soul or get in anyone's way. It'll be the easiest money the old guy's ever made. Scout's honor

OMG 😳

I've worked with her long enough to know the straw's cracking the camel's back.

> Don't worry about it. Sometimes no really means no 🙁

Who am I fooling? I never take "no" for an answer.

THREE

CHASE

E ldon and I finish pushing the cattle into the barn to weather the approaching storm. Shadowy clouds menace the sky, drawing closer, and forecasts have temperatures dropping into the single digits.

Thankfully, Maddie's winter break starts today, buying us a couple of solid weeks without worrying about snow chains, bus stops, and all of that. I have half a mind to pick her up in the sleigh this afternoon. The kids at her bus stop will get a kick out of that.

Eldon stiffly jumps down from his mount, chewing a piece of straw between his teeth. Nodding towards one of the heifers, he remarks, "Chase, my gut tells me this one's about to calve."

Sizing her up for a long moment, I have to agree. We had a couple of new ranch hands last spring, and there was an incident with the electric fencing and one of the bulls getting out of his enclosure and into the herd. Fortunately, when the vet came out to do preg checks, only this one came up positive.

I shake my head, still ruing the needlessness of the situation. "It would have to happen in the middle of a blizzard. We better separate her and make things nice and cozy for her."

After we've got Mama relocated away from the herd in a separate area with fresh, dry straw, we feed and water the cattle, offering extra grain and winter wheat to help the animals stay warm. I double-check the heater, ensuring it's in good working order and free of fire hazards. We use it for the smaller animals wintering over in the barn, including laying hens and roosters, goats, pigs, and turkeys. But it'll come in handy with the calf, too.

"I'll stay out in the barn tonight. Just in case," Eldon offers.

"We'll take shifts," I reply. "But first things first. What are your thoughts about fetching that Christmas tree before the storm rolls in?" I ask, side-eyeing the old man. Hours of fence mending have given me time to reflect on my childhood, remembering the vital importance of Christmas in my youth. How can I deny Maddie those experiences? Especially after what she's been through.

A big smile lights his face. "Maddie'll love it, and so will Véronique." Véronique does basic cooking and cleaning for us, and I've long suspected Eldon, a lifelong bachelor, has a thing for her.

I grumble, still not wanting to push this Christmas festivity stuff too far, "Maybe the girls can whip up some cookies and other baked goods. And we've got the ham to smoke for Christmas dinner. It'll undoubtedly have a Basque flavor, like everything else."

Véronique's the daughter of French-Basque immigrants, and her cooking and cleaning skills were highly valued during Lisa's prolonged illness. I know Maddie craves her feminine presence, although nothing can replace her mama. "And I guess we'll make it festive for the other ranch hands, too. Anybody staying around the bunkhouse over the holiday?"

Eldon answers as we work together to close the barn doors. "Apart from Avery and me, no. Everyone's either headed down to Ouray or wherever their family hales from. That means Chihuahua for Jose, Raul, and their kin and Texas for Keaton, Lyle, and Dexter." The cowboy shivers against the cold, adding, "The way this storm's blowing in, I should split for Mexico, too."

"Don't think too much on that, old-timer."

"Margaritas, warm weather, pretty beaches, prettier señoritas. I made a mistake..."

"The only drink sipping we'll be doing is eggnog. Ready to go get that tree?"

"Sure thing, Boss."

Heading to the stables, we leave our mounts with Avery, the stable hand with a mop of black, curly hair who's worked with us since graduating high school last spring. Like all eighteen year-olds, he's morose and introverted, which suits me perfectly. The last thing I need is the expectation of making conversation in the stables. Besides, the kid can muck a stall and tack a horse, which is all I care about.

I point at the teen. "You staying in the stables with the horses during the blizzard?"

"Yes, sir." He pulls a white corded earphone from his ear, making me second guess what he heard.

"We'll run a rope from the stables to the main house for dinners and such, so you don't get turned around or lost if this blizzard comes in as hard as they're forecasting."

He nods.

Wheeling around, I stride towards the restored black

and red antique horse-drawn Albany cutter sleigh. It lies buried beneath a thick dust-covered canvas to protect the red velvet upholstery. Pulling back the cover, I run a hand over the glossy black surface. She brings back countless childhood Christmas memories.

I order Avery, "The draft horses, son." He nods, quickly bringing out the black and gray mottled Percherons. Soon, Eldon and I fly across the snowy landscape to the soft thud of massive horse hooves and the faint tinkle of bells.

The storm's nearly upon us when we find and cut the perfect specimen, an eight-foot lodgepole pine with a stately spread of green branches.

"Good thing you pulled out the sleigh because I wouldn't want to drive the truck down to the mailboxes in this weather," Eldon remarks, his teeth chattering.

Mine are, too. I make a mental note to grab some blankets before heading down to the bus stop. Fortunately, it's just past the long driveway exiting the property at the mailboxes; we won't be outside much longer.

The sky transforms from dark and menacing to a disorienting swirl of icy flakes. By their size and speed, this storm front won't let up anytime soon. I glance at my watch— nearly time to head to the bus stop.

Sloshing through several weeks' worth of snow back to the house, the majestic beauty of the wintry landscape and the intimate stillness of the snowstorm captivate me. At the ranch's side entry, Eldon and I shuffle out, wrestling the tree into the mudroom to thaw.

"I sure hope every critter's out of there," Eldon says, shoving his hands in his back pockets and kicking at the ground where melting snow drips. Usually, we'd set it outside for a while to ensure the squirrels, birds, and mice depart. But not in this weather. "Can't imagine Maddie and

Véronique handling rodents skittering through the house well. Or owls flying between the rafters."

I shrug. "Wouldn't be the first time." Ranch life comes with plenty of animals.

Heading back to the sleigh, I tease, "Besides, you can act as Véronique's knight in shining armor. It'll go a long way towards breaking the ice."

Eldon lets out a puff of air that freezes in the afternoon light, swept away in a swirl of fluffy snowflakes. "There'll be no ice-breaking between Véronique and me, although she is lovely."

"A lovely woman who could use a little Christmas company."

The old man's shoulders rise and fall dramatically, and I fight the booming laugh that grips my chest. *Just as I thought.* "What, don't tell me you're afraid to be alone in the same house with her while I go to get Maddie? Do you need to ride along?"

"Enough of your tee-heeing," he grumbles, frowning. But it's the kind of straining frown that'll turn into a smile the moment his concentration breaks. Despite the teasing, Eldon stays back, offering to help Véronique unload boxes of ornaments and decorations from the ample space underneath the great room's giant staircase.

Clomping towards the bus stop, I pull my Carhartt collar up against the chill of the wind. A more powerful onslaught of frigid gusts assaults me, cold, icy fingers of wind stealing through the blankets I snatched from the old wooden steamer chest in the living room. Fortunately, I had enough sense to replace my cowboy hat with a knit cap.

A red Honda Civic breaks the monotony of the white landscape ahead. As I get closer, I see it slid off the side of the road into one of the large drainage ditches lining the long driveway to the ranch. That's going to be a costly mistake for the driver.

Drawing closer, a lithe female form emerges wrapped in a buttery, beige leather coat with white fur trim and bulky red mittens sticking out of her pockets. Furry snow boots hug her feet and calves, and black knit pants enhance the curves of her legs. The leggings belong in a yoga class—not a blizzard.

She paces back and forth, her lovely brows knit together. A mane of blonde tresses flow from a blue knit cap to the middle of her back. Her hands look beet-red from the bite of the air, although she keeps her mittens off, frantically typing on her phone.

I stop the sleigh beside her, remarking, "I hate to break this to you, ma'am, but good luck getting a cellphone signal out here."

She looks up, her warm, soulful brown eyes catching mine, and I work hard to silence the strangled sound that rises in my throat—Chanel Love. I furrow my brows, bobbling my head between her ditch-bound vehicle and the long driveway to my home. My heart races as I strain to string two words together. She's easily ten times more radiant and beautiful in person, and I feel like a man sunk up to his neck in quicksand with no rope or branch in sight.

The smile on her face doesn't reach her warm cinnamon-hued eyes, and her voice sounds raw. "I have AAA, but I need a cell signal. Don't you people have satellite cell phone coverage?"

You people. The surge of anger those two words excite help me regain my tattered composure. "Look, I can give you a lift back to my place, if you like? You can use the phone there to call your boyfriend or husband. But honestly, you're not getting your vehicle towed in this

19

weather." My eyes drop to the California license plate peeking out of the snow. Most likely a rental, but I do remember reading online about California inspiring her work. From fluffy, useless snow boots to her fashionable rather than functional jacket, she's got city girl written all over her. I'd wager the Bay Area or Southern California.

She raises an eyebrow, blurting out, "Boyfriend. That's funny."

"Why?" There's nothing about her appearance that exudes *single* to me. Yet, I notice, with a strange satisfaction, that her left hand bears no ring.

She shrugs.

"Well, you've got my curiosity up now, ma'am. Do go on."

"Not that I need to tell you any of this, but my ex said I was a cold-hearted...let's go with 'ice princess.'" She puts air quotes around the last two words, her cheeks bright from the bracing breeze.

"A real-life ice princess, huh?" My eyebrows shoot up, and I tug on my collar to shield my neck. She does look like a princess—fine and feminine, her big doe eyes staring up at me. I can only imagine her expression when she figures out what I already know.

No tow truck on the planet'll go out in this weather, and the closest ranch is hundreds of acres away. Chanel Love's finally got her wish—a stay at Heart's Desire that'll last as long as this storm. I shake my head, muttering to myself. She doesn't know what she's done.

The romance writer grimaces, pressing her pretty lips into a sad bow. "I shouldn't have told you any of that. But the whole ice princess thing is kind of a constant refrain from past boyfriends, *in case you're wondering*." She bites her lower lip, making my heart strain in my chest. "I know you're not."

Oh, yes, I am.

"At the risk of you turning into a real ice princess, how about I give you that lift?"

Her eyes narrow, scrutinizing me. Her mouth opens, and I'm certain she's about to ask for my name.

Not ready for *that* conversation, I glance at my watch. I'm moments away from the bus's arrival. "Hold that thought," I say, urging the horses forward.

FOUR

CHANEL

He rode off and left me? Seriously?!?!

For a moment, the man almost reminded me of one of the heroes in my romances—rugged, untamed, and riding to the rescue. Only without the cowboy hat. But he abandoned me despite the stunning golden-green eyes, the large build, and the rugged square-set jaw enhanced by a chestnut-colored beard.

Is he coming back? Will I freeze to death? What does "hold that thought" even mean?

Chivalry is dead. Finito. Gone.

Panic grips me as I wonder what will happen if the sleigh driver doesn't return. Maybe forgets about me altogether? How long until my fingers and toes freeze?

I wrap my arms tightly around myself, my fur-lined leather jacket, red mittens, and blue knit cap no match for the blustery wind. And as for my two hundred dollar, fur-trimmed snow boots? My toes feel stiff and frozen inside. "Seriously, cute boots? You had one job."

The wind increases, announced by the stiffness of my entire body and the uncontrollable chattering of my teeth.

And flurries of snow whip and twirl around me, declaring the obvious. Mr. Gorgeous has abandoned me smack-dab in the middle of a blizzard in remote Colorado with no cell phone signal. Great!

My pity party builds steam, the only thing keeping me warm, until a soft jingling of bells in the distance catches my ear. It grows in frequency and intensity, putting a tight knot of hope in my chest. Maybe Mother Nature hasn't conspired to turn the ice princess into an icicle after all.

Straining my eyes, I make out distant gray forms that transform into the sleek black and red sleigh with the massive horses and the vanishing sleigh driver. A smaller form snuggles in the blankets beside him, the composite sight making my eyes water and my heart warm. Or maybe it's the cold finishing me off.

Sylvia told me I should set my next series in Texas, not Colorado. Maybe the universe is trying to tell me something. I'll get a ride from Mr. Gorgeous, beg, borrow, or steal my way out of this snowy prison and *never look back*. Whatever you want, Universe. I'll do anything. Just please get me out of here.

The sleigh stops next to me, and the man jumps down without hesitation, heading in my direction with one of the blankets. My eyes round, surprised by the sudden change in his demeanor. He wraps the blanket around my shoulders, frowning. "I didn't want to miss the school bus. And I needed a few minutes to think about the predicament you've gotten yourself in."

"And?" The wind whips around us like a snowy vortex, the storm's calm eye centered between us. "Let's get you situated and warming up. Then, we can talk. Do you have luggage in your car or anything I need to grab?"

I checked out of my hotel earlier, ready to leave Ouray

behind for good after my last-ditch attempt to visit the ranch. "Yes." I shuffle through my coat pocket for my keys.

"Let's get you warming in the sleigh first."

I nod, taking his big hand wrapped in a rugged leather work glove. The snow proves deceptively deep in spots, thanks to drifts and uneven terrain.

I slide sideways on a slippery patch, but the large man stops me, wrapping his robust arm around my waist and hoisting me the rest of the way to the sleigh. I feel instantly warmer, thoroughly impressed by his strength and steady feet. He helps me step up at the sleigh, providing an extra boost with his hands around my waist. I go from chattering teeth to burning cheeks in a heartbeat.

The little girl eyes me enthusiastically, flashing a big, toothy grin. Thick brown fringe frames her periwinkle eyes, containing the clarity and sparkle of diamonds. I sit on the red velvet upholstery next to her, fishing out my keys and handing them to Mr. Gorgeous.

He looks up at me questioningly, his stunning amber and moss eyes swirling warmly. "I have two purple bags in the trunk and my purse in the driver's seat. Thank you."

He nods, sauntering towards the vehicle. My mind swirls with what I need, and I call after him, "My laptop bag on the front passenger seat should come, too, and..." I think about the five new coffee table books in the trunk, deciding to leave them in the car. They should be fine. But my copy needs to come. "And there's a coffee table book next to the laptop bag. I'd really appreciate it if you can keep the snow off it. It's precious to me." Bringing the blankets up to my chin and letting out a shivering breath, I rub my mittens together, trying to warm up.

The little girl eyes me curiously. I call out over the howl of the wind, "Is it always this cold here?"

Her eyes dance, and her cheeks glow ruddy from the chill. "Yes, all winter long. Do you like the snow?"

The girl's innocent question catches me off guard, forcing me to pause and notice my surroundings. Despite the sheer winds and the wild snowflakes twirling and swirling around us, the savage beauty of this place is incomparable.

I work hard to etch it in my brain. Nature's icy, chaotic winter dance would create a beautiful romance novel setting. One where the hero rescues the heroine, takes her back to his cozy cabin, and they fall madly in love. Sighing and craning my neck, I realize the little girl's waiting raptly for my answer. "I do like the snow."

"Great!" she exclaims with a giggle. "I like building snowmen. How about you?"

"Yes, I love building snowmen and snowwomen, too."

"Snowwomen?" she questions, twisting her face. "Never heard of such a thing!"

"They have braids made of woven straw and skirts made from horse blankets. At least they always did on my grandparents' ranch."

"And eyes and smiles made with stones and carrot noses?"

I eye her with pretend suspicion. "For someone who claims she's never heard of snowwomen, you seem to know an awful lot about them."

She giggles and covers her mouth. "I do, don't I?"

Out of the corner of my eye, I see the burly man pause, my luggage in hand, and a strange look on his face as he watches the little girl and me. I wish I knew him better to guess his thoughts.

"My name's Maddie. What's yours?" the little girl

hollers over the wind, as fascinated by the great puffs of white leaving her mouth as any answer I might give.

"I'm Chanel," I say, offering my mittened hand to her gloved one.

"You're pretty," she says, forming her lips into a crooked grin. "Like a princess."

I push a stray hair back from her warm cheek. "You're pretty, too."

The man looks up into the sleigh again, hesitantly assessing our interaction.

Maddie's face suddenly goes mischievous as she asks, "Do you think my daddy's handsome?"

My cheeks instantly darken as the candid question reminds me that kids have no filters. I can tell by the way the man suddenly looks down but lingers where he stands that he heard the question and wants an answer, too.

My heart pounds against my ribcage. Reminding myself I'm talking to a little girl who admires her father, I reply, "Yes, your daddy is very handsome."

He starts moving again after that, working with a newfound rapidity and energy that makes me smile. There's no other way to describe him, from his Carhartt jacket to his Wranglers and neatly trimmed brown beard.

"How old are you, Maddie?" I scream. The wind whips around us, seemingly angry we persist in chatting.

"Ten, and how about you, Chanel?"

"Thirty-two."

"My dad's forty-two," she says, quirking her mouth and bobbing her head back and forth between us. I get the impression her dad is single, and she's a matchmaker. But who knows with kids?

The driver climbs fluidly into the sleigh, urging the horses forward to the tinkling of bells. Projecting his voice, he says, "I locked up your car, and everything should be safe until this blows over." He hands me the keys, and I put them back in my coat pocket.

"Thank you. Did you get the book?" *Why does the question sound breathless?*

He nods, narrowing his eyes and patting his chest. "It's under my jacket to keep the snow out. "What's so special about it?"

That's a good question. Unable to say more than a few intelligible words, thanks to the whipping wind, sloshing horse hooves, sleigh bells, and distance between us, I yell, "It's my inspiration."

His face grows unreadable as he knits his brows, looking toward the team of horses and no longer trying to make conversation.

FIVE

CHANEL

M addie snuggles next to me, grabbing my left hand beneath the blankets and holding it with both of hers. "How did you meet my daddy?"

"My car got stuck in the snow, and he saved me."

Her face beams with pride. "He's good at doing stuff like that!" she exclaims.

"That must be nice to have a daddy who specializes in saving people. Is he like a superhero or something?" I'm being silly now, trying to make her laugh. But from the look of his build, he could be in law enforcement, a firefighter, the military, or maybe an EMT.

She giggles. "Yes, he's super daddy!"

The man's eyes glide back and forth between the little girl and me, ambivalence in his expression like he's trying to process the situation. I wonder if he's married, which is impossible to ascertain thanks to his leather gloves. I can't imagine him single with that achingly attractive, chiseled face and tall, rugged frame.

Maddie says in a loud whisper, "You *do* like my daddy. You keep staring at him!"

My cheeks darken, and I shake my head. Whether the man hears or not, he doesn't respond, keeping his eyes forward. I silently thank him for the polite gesture. "You're a very silly girl. So, what's your favorite part of Christmas?"

Her face grows serious, and her eyes swim with tears. "We don't really celebrate Christmas anymore."

My heart sinks, all-too-familiar waves of disappointment crashing into me. I could be talking to myself at that age. I look past her at Mr. Gorgeous, and at the same moment, he turns to face us. I don't know if he caught his daughter's words, but sadness shrouds his guarded face, piquing my curiosity. Yet, his eyes overflow with warmth and curiosity as if he's finally decided to embrace my interactions with his little girl.

"Do *you* celebrate Christmas?" she asks, pulling my eyes from her dad's tender gaze.

"It's one of my favorite times of the year now. I celebrate with my friends back home. We get together and go to dinner or watch movies and exchange gifts. Sometimes, we dress up in ugly sweaters and do fun things like go to the Boat Parade in Newport Beach. But when I was your age, I didn't celebrate, either."

She nods, snuggling into me. "Maybe we could try celebrating together. How long are you planning on staying?"

I laugh, trying to wrap my head around adolescence again. How liberating for everything to be so simple. Unlike Maddie, who's already settled happily into the presence of a total stranger at her house for the holidays, my head swims with denial, dreaming up increasingly outlandish ways to escape my current predicament.

Despite the idyllic nature of this winter adventure, I have a flight to catch, books to finish, book signings to attend, and conferences to present at. The list is never-ending, and it doesn't include a Colorado Christmas.

Mr. Gorgeous barks gruffly. "That's enough questions for the moment, pipsqueak. Our guest still has a lot to figure out. And everything will depend on the weather. Maybe we'll get lucky, and a Christmas miracle will happen. That way, we can get California back home where she belongs."

Maddie frowns dramatically.

But his new nickname perks up my ears. "Why California?" I ask, feeling like I'm missing something.

"It was on your license plate."

That's right. I nod. "That's a rental car, though."

"So, you're from?"

I explain, "No, I am from California. But that isn't my car."

He nods. "We're almost to the ranch now. We'll set you up in front of the fireplace with blankets and a hot drink to take the blue tinge off your lips."

"Really?" I say, touching a mitten reflexively to my mouth.

He shakes his head. "That was a joke."

"Hard to tell with your perpetual frown and deadpan expression."

He opens his mouth to speak, but Maddie chimes in, "Daddy never smiles anymore."

My eyes wander back to his questioningly. Instead of providing context, he looks forward, concentrating hard on the reigns, an activity he made look effortless only moments before. I catch myself, holding my breath as my eyes follow the straight line of his nose down to his generous, kissable lips, and strong chin.

"You're staring at Daddy again!" Maddie squeals,

sending my gaze skittering guiltily into the blinding white of the blizzard.

Loudly clearing his throat, the man draws my gaze back toward his face. He winks, his mouth turning up ever so slightly at the corners. "She may only be ten, but she's already a perpetual romantic, something I imagine you know a little about."

I arch an eyebrow. "Wait, what do you mean?" I can only guess he's referring to my romance writing. Does he recognize me or something?

Questions abound, but nature won't cooperate. The howling of the wind grows to a fevered pitch, sounding dangerously alive and angry.

Following the man's lead, I look forward at the horses. The girl snuggles closer, and I wrap my arm around her, reveling in the adorableness of her cherub-plump cheeks. *Is this what it's like to have a daughter?*

The man side-eyes us, his face relaxing, like he's growing accustomed to us together. I could almost read relief in his expression, but I don't know him well enough to be sure.

In the distance, faint lights glimmer, announcing a massive, rough-hewn two-story cabin. It looks like a smaller version of the Old Faithful Inn in Yellowstone National Park, with its wooden shingled sides and multi-gabled roof. I wonder if the inside's as cozy.

Suddenly, it hits me. Despite the snow obscuring my view, *this* is Heart's Desire Ranch.

The little girl smiles up at me, excitement flooding her face. She screams over the wind and the storm, "Now, winter break begins! No more school for me. Yippee!"

I shake my head, wondering how Mr. Gorgeous fits into the mix. Maybe he's an employee who lives here year-round with his family? A ranch hand or perhaps the ranch foreman? After all, he does exude a quiet authority. My mind races with possibilities, and my heart drums, realizing I may finally be on the verge of meeting Chase Heart.

Deep breaths, Chanel. Keep it together.

The sleigh stops in front of the massive ranch house, and I watch the driver jump down athletically, offering the girl his hand. Once on the ground, Maddie motions to him, and he squats down in the snow. She screams loud enough for me to hear, "She's beautiful, Daddy. Like a princess."

He strokes his beard pensively, grumbling, "Elsa or Belle?"

Maddie laughs, covering her mouth with her white-gloved hand before blurting out, "Elsa."

Sizing me up with his perpetual frown, the sleigh driver nods. "I couldn't agree more. After all, she told me herself. She has an ice palace she hides in somewhere around here."

I furrow my brow, and he laughs. The unexpected sound personifies masculine gorgeousness, resonant and deep, putting a knot in my throat. I would like to hear more of it. Hugging the little girl, he says, "Get inside and help with the ornaments. We've got a tree to decorate, sweetie."

"A tree!" she shrieks enthusiastically. It strikes me as a little too excited for a ten-year-old. Coupled with her earlier revelation that they don't celebrate Christmas, I have more questions than answers.

To the man I call, "Elsa, huh?"

He nods, straightening up and coming around the side of the sleigh to offer me his gloved hand. "Yes, ma'am. You said it yourself, and you are wearing gloves. But you know how I know for sure?"

I begrudgingly frown.

"Most eyes shoot daggers when angry, but yours prefer

shards of ice, no less dangerous but much colder. I saw it myself when I raced off on the sleigh earlier."

I roll my eyes, none too amused. "I thought you left me."

"Whoa, whoa! There will be no eye rolling around this household," he scolds, trying to make his face stern even though a merriment dances beneath the surface. "I've gotten by a decade without seeing that from Maddie. No introducing a bad habit now."

"Don't say silly things to make me roll them then." Grabbing his strong hand, I jump down to the ground, doddering and slipping on impact, thanks to my stupid boots.

He reflexively grabs my waist with his other arm, steadying me. For one delicious moment, we stand face to face and chest to chest, the white puffs from our fast-paced breathing swirling into one frosty cloud.

Staring down at me, he adds, "And for the record, I would never leave you anywhere, although I might make you wait for a bit."

The words steal my breath. But a moment later, he pulls his warm arm from my waist, leaving me frigid. His face and body language become formal, putting distance between us, but his hand continues to hold my mittened one. Clearing his throat, he says, "Time to dethaw you by the fireplace."

"Thank you," I say, my eyes rising to take in the stunning two-story ranch house before me. "For saving my life."

He nods. Pausing, his gaze washes over my face. "It's even more beautiful inside." The left corner of his mouth sneaks upward into something approaching a lopsided grin. A dimple emerges above the edge of his beard, and my heart stutters. I look down to conceal my glowing cheeks, savoring how he holds my hand up the massive stone stairs and into the house, well past the point of needing to steady me in the snow.

Unlike Olivier, who claimed to be a gentleman, Mr. Gorgeous is the real deal, his earlier abandonment via sleigh aside. But he came back...with a good excuse.

A warm blast of air hits me as we enter the house, walking into a massive great room in the Arts and Crafts style. Rich, warm, polished wood planks line the walls horizontally, and a gigantic hearth constructed from local granite boulders draws my attention to the center of the room. The fire inside glows and crackles, filling the enormous space with cozy, alpine charm.

My eyes follow the vaulted ceiling of the great room to its lofty two-story peak. Soaring, rough-hewn wooden rafters fashioned from sinewy lengths of wood brought to a glossy shine greet me. My breath catches in my throat as I survey the wrap-around balcony of the second floor, a masterpiece of rustic construction.

"May I take your hat and gloves?" The attentive man asks, and I hand them to him, still distracted by our stunning surroundings. Our bare fingers accidentally touch and sparks zing from his warm, work-hardened fingertips to my colder, softer ones, making me exhale softly.

He swallows audibly, licking his lips and fighting what continues to look more and more like an actual smile. Stepping forward, my snow boots tap on the wooden floorboards, as my eyes stretch to take in opulent textiles on the walls. Native American-patterned throws accent rugged, handmade couches, and breathtaking carpets in rich jewel-toned designs glow against the ancient wood flooring.

With one powerful stride, the man snags my fingertips with his, leading me lightly forward toward a big, overstuffed chair in front of the fireplace. Sparks trail from his flesh up my arm, doing far more to warm me than any fire. Staring up, I finally see a neat row of big, white teeth framed by two dimples my fingers ache to touch.

"Have a seat," he invites in low tones, pushing me closer to the hearth before grabbing a super soft Native American print blanket and tucking me into the chair. I haven't felt this secure since before my mom left my dad. It brings me closer to tears than I care to admit.

"Let me grab your belongings before this weather gets ahead of us. And Véronique can work on a hot drink for you." He looks over the chair, making eye contact with someone behind me. I twist to the left to peer around the chair's high back, where a plump woman with short salt and pepper hair stands, wearing a red apron. She nods business-like at me.

Next to her, a rugged older man with an extravagant handlebar mustache stands. His silver eyes dance warmly, and an infectious smile captures my lips. I would know him anywhere—Chase Heart!

He's exactly as I pictured, every bit as rugged and stately in his advanced cowboy age. My heart soars, recognizing an artistic soulmate as the man removes his hat, revealing thinning, unkempt gray hair as he gives me a polite, though stiff, bow.

SIX

CHASE

Returning from the storm for a second time, my arms laden with luggage, a high-pitched squeal grabs my attention.

Setting down the purple bags, I fully expect to see my daughter in the middle of some mischievous act. Instead, my eyes rest on Chanel, standing beside the high-backed chair with her hand over her mouth.

Tears roll down her cheeks, but her face betrays no sadness. My head spins at the incongruence, and I cross the distance to her, confused by what could change her mood so quickly. Her eyes snap excitedly, and the hand over her mouth trembles slightly. I would give more than I'm willing to admit to see her look at me that way—just once.

But I might as well be chopped liver because every ounce of her being and energy centers squarely on Eldon. *What in the world is going on?*

Véronique's eyes narrow, shooting daggers at the blonde whose countenance can only be described as adoring. Chanel fans her face with her hand now, saying aloud, "I told myself I wouldn't do this. But yes, even best-selling authors fangirl when they finally meet their favorite poet and artist in the world. Especially after giving up all hope it would ever happen."

Favorite poet and artist in the world? What in the world?

Shuffling up next to me as she swipes her hands over her moist cheeks, she whispers, "I hope I don't have mascara everywhere?"

In one trip to the sleigh, I've gone from a handsome rescuer to a stand-in mirror. This has to rank somewhere in the outfield of the friend zone with my back against the fence.

Shouldn't her sudden disinterest please me? After all I've done to avoid meeting this woman? Instead, I feel an odd mixture of resentment and envy.

If that's not enough, she shrugs, asking me, "Where's the book?"

Oh, you mean my book? I fight hard to keep the words from toppling from my lips. After all, I'm still trying to wrap my head around what's going on. Frowning deeply, I unzip my Carhartt, producing the warm book, and hand it to her.

"Thank you," Ms. Sunshine replies, beelining straight past me like I don't exist. The room suddenly feels like it's all about Eldon and Chanel. Only the old man looks as puzzled as the rest of us, and Véronique seethes. Maddie and Avery are in the mudroom, making some commotion over the Christmas tree. But I ignore it, too absorbed by this odd moment to think about anything else.

Crossing the distance to the rugged ranch hand, the blonde takes his hand, shaking it enthusiastically. "My name is Chanel Montgomery, and I'm your biggest fan. Okay, not like a Stephen King *Misery* creepy kind of fan. But you know, the good kind who loves your poems and artwork and can't get enough of them. I know this seems odd because you don't even know me, and I have the impression you may not want to meet me. But I feel like we're kindred spirits in some way. You know, as fellow writers."

Eldon's bushy eyebrows climb his wizened forehead, and I bite my lip, trying hard not to laugh or say something. The old man shoots me a quizzical look, and I shake my head, urging him to play along for just a tad longer.

Something tells me the most forthright Chanel will ever be regarding my work is with someone else. And all of a sudden, I desperately need to know what she thinks of my work.

But then, a twinge of guilt grips me. I need to end this before it gets ugly. I holler in her direction, "What are you doing bothering that grumpy, old cowboy?" I hope the allusion will stop her in her tracks, allowing me to fess up before things spiral out of control.

But nope, the author's searching the great room for a pen, ready to make the old guy sign her book. Véronique's face looks as red as the lobsters she boils for us on special occasions, and she twists her fists in her apron. Suddenly, the cook storms out of the room, her face clouded with confusion.

"What's gotten into her?" Eldon asks, still looking awestruck by the whole situation.

"Jealousy," I reply flatly, looking at Chanel. I know exactly how Véronique feels.

The pretty author's mouth forms a perfect pink bow that I long to do more than look at, and she says, "Oh no, it's not like that. She has nothing to be jealous of. I'm just doing a little fangirling. That's all."

"Yeah, she does have reason to be jealous," I say, stepping forward with a frown. "Because as far as she's concerned, there's no reason for you to be fawning over this guy."

Chanel shakes her head, confused.

Turning to Eldon, I say, "Why don't you go after Véronique? Calm her down a bit."

"How do I do that?" The lifelong bachelor asks, his hands tightly folded in front of him.

"By listening more than talking and complimenting her every chance you get. Good luck, old man."

The wrinkly ranch hand leaves the room, shaking his head. My heart races as I look at Chanel, reaching into my back pocket and pulling out my wallet.

She eyes me with growing confusion. "Did I say something wrong?" she asks, her head swiveling back and forth between me and the entrance to the kitchen.

Letting out a low sigh, I steel myself for this revelation and the pleasurable conversation to follow. If I get even half the show she put on for Eldon, I'll be a happy man, though I still refuse to admit how much I need Chanel's attention. "Here," I say, handing her my driver's license."

She takes it, knitting her eyebrows as her eyes streak between my face and the laminated card. I wait for it to sink in. The cute little puff of air to escape her mouth with a high-pitched sound, her hand to cover her mouth and her eyes to dance, her handshake and compliments about my poems and art and what they mean to her.

Instead, she shoves the license into my chest, making me scramble to grab it from her tiny hands. Putting her fists on her hips and glaring at me, she spits, "I suppose you think all of this is funny, huh?"

Kind of, but I don't see that answer going over well. "Look—" I start, but she smacks my arm, her eyes seething.

Gone are the ice shards, replaced by livid streams of molten lava.

"So, you're Chase Heart? You're Chase Heart?" Her voice climbs an octave as she repeats the question. Rubbing her hands over her face, she lets out something approaching a growl, but because of the dainty femininity she exudes, it comes across more like a kitten hissing—completely adorable.

I'll say one thing about Chanel Love, I mean Montgomery. She doesn't give me a spare second to start feeling guilty about my attraction to her or ruminating over my fear of loss. Every moment with her is like a crazy roller-coaster ride, with me hanging on for dear life.

"And you're Chanel Montgomery—*not Love*."

"Oh no, you don't," she yells, waggling her finger in my face. That's my pen name. It's not remotely the same as purposefully concealing your identity."

"Purposefully concealing my identity from you? How so?"

"By making me think the guy with the mustache was you."

"His name's Eldon, and I beg your pardon. I did not make you think anything of the sort. That was you coming to your own conclusions."

She shakes her head, smacking my chest again. "You have no online presence, only one photo from the back wearing a hat and duster, *and*, based on your earlier comment, I'm pretty darn sure you had something to do with the 'grumpy, old cowboy' rumor circulating Ouray."

I look down, chuckling under my breath. "It's a running joke. Has been for a long time. After all, you've met me. What was *your* first impression?"

She's still got her fists on her hips, but now she adds

toe-tapping to the mix. Standing in this pose, pink with anger, the fiery blonde is something I never want to forget. If she lets me live long enough to remember.

Finally, she splutters, "Grumpy *young* cowboy. That was my first impression of you, and hopefully, it'll be my last." Her words sting more than they should.

Chanel rubs her hands over her face. "Where can I get a little privacy and make a phone call?"

"Are you really trying to tell me there's no part of you happy to meet me?" I ask, deflated.

She shakes her head defiantly.

Ouch! "Really?" I grab my book, which she's gone from reverently holding to tossing haphazardly in the high-backed chair. "So these words and these pictures no longer mean the same thing because I don't meet your expectations as an author?"

"Not only are you absolutely, one hundred percent not the man I think of as Chase Heart, but you just made me look like a fool in front of everybody."

"I did no such thing—"

"Please, I'm tired, and it's been a long day. Could you just show me to my room?"

"Okay," I shrug, numb with frustration. "But even though you didn't care for the author reveal, I'm still the same man who wrote and drew the things you claim to love."

She lets her head fall back, sighing long and loud as she stares at the ceiling. The fury pouring off the formerly sunshiny woman couldn't be more palpable—deadly as solar flares.

"Let me show you to your room. There's a landline in there," I grumble, feeling colder by the minute. It's about time I headed out to check on the heifer anyway.

A new kind of guilt grips me, thinking back on Chanel's promises to Maddie on the sleigh ride. The little girl's going to be beyond disappointed when she realizes Chanel's no longer in the mood for Christmas fun.

As I lead the woman upstairs to the guest bedroom, carrying a purple bag in each hand, I search for a way to turn the evening around. Remind her about the Christmas date she has with my daughter, even if she never wants to see or talk to me again. Words couldn't fail me at a more crucial time. Standing in front of the door to her bedroom, I observe gruffly, "Dinner's in an hour."

She scowls at me.

"You should eat. I'm sure you burned up a lot of calories standing out there in the cold today."

She nods begrudgingly, ending the conversation by shutting the door. I stand there, staring at the knots in the wood, rubbing my hand over my heart and etching the habitual frown back into my face.

I tried, Lisa. But see what I mean? I'm just not cut out for this second chance love stuff.

SEVEN

CHANEL

T he walls and floors of the well-appointed guest room feature rich wood planking like the great room and a mini version of the stone hearth downstairs with a gas fire. A large four-poster bed accented with thick blue, purple, white, and black Amish quilts welcomes me, and I beeline for it, crumpling into an exhausted heap.

My head spins, trying to make sense of what just happened. How in the world could I have been so wrong about Chase Heart? Instead of my safe little old cowboy, he's... Oh my goodness, what is he? Gorgeous, masculine, towering, and soulfully, wonderfully made.

"God, how could you do this to me?" I ask into the silence of the room. "I mean, he's perfect for me...like terrifyingly, handsomely, mind-bogglingly perfect. His daughter is adorable, and he isn't wearing a ring." Guilt tugs at me for checking, but I had to know, even in my rage-induced state.

I feel like a total fool. Not so much for mistaking Eldon for Chase but for making a royal scene in response. "How hard would it have been to laugh off the whole thing, Chanel? Instead, you turned it into something ugly and awkward."

I have to get out of here. I can't stay one moment longer. I check my cell phone, still seeing no bars. Picking up the cordless phone by the bed, I dial Sylvia's number.

"Hello?" she answers, no doubt thrown off by the unrecognized number.

"Sylvia, it's me."

"Oh good. I tried to call you earlier, but you didn't pick up."

"Yeah, it's a long story. What's going on?"

"You sound like you've been crying. Are you okay?"

I sniffle, rubbing my sleeve over my face. "Yeah," I lie, trying to sound cheery. "It was just a really long day."

"Anything you want to talk about?"

"No." *Talk about a bald-faced lie!*

"Okay, well, I just wanted to go over ad performance with you for the past couple of days and confirm the most recent version of *Love's Yearning* you emailed me is the final, final, final draft going out to ARC readers and reviewers."

"Yep."

"Oh, and I need more guidance about what you want the Street Team to do this month."

Inhaling deeply, I steady my voice. "Let's save the ad performance for later. My brain's too scattered for number crunching right now. Yes, use the last version I emailed you. Umm...what was the other thing again?"

"Street Team."

"Right. Have them keep building momentum around the *Love's Yearning* launch."

"You have been crying. I'm certain of it now."

Despite my best efforts, a sob wrenches my chest.

"Oh, honey, what's wrong?"

I inhale sharply. "Remember how you advised me to give up on the whole Heart's Desire thing and leave the family alone? Well—"

"Well…" her voice sits somewhere between recrimination and amusement.

"I kind of decided to drive out to the ranch. You know, beg in person and hope Mr. Heart wouldn't have me arrested for trespassing."

"Oh Chanel…" Sylvia's voice slides up a whole step. "Do you need bail money?"

"No," I half sob, half giggle. Leave it to Sylvia to point out how much worse it could be. "But I might as well be in prison. The weather got crazy on the drive over, and then I had an altercation with the drainage ditch on one side of his monumentally long driveway."

She gasps.

"Fortunately, Chase spirited me in a horse-drawn sleigh back to his place to wait out the storm. But everyone here seems to think it could go on for days, which means I'm going to miss my flight and all of my events for this next week—"

"Okay, hold it right there. You finally met Chase Heart? Tell me everything."

"What do you want to know?"

"*Everything*. His age, his appearance, what's the deal with him being so mysterious online?"

I frown, struggling with how to describe him. "He's a bit younger than I thought…"

"So, like mid-fifties or sixties?"

"Forty-two."

"Ohh," she replies, a new lilt to her voice. "And how is he on the eyes?"

I let out a long exhale. "Attractive, but only if you're into grumpy single dads..."

She hyperventilates. "Umm...one hundred percent! How many kids does he have?"

"One daughter named Maddie. She's ten and adorable."

"And why are you crying again?"

"Because he's not what I expected. I'll explain the rest later, but I need to get out of here. Like this instant. Whether it's hiring a Snowcat, dogsled team, alpine search and rescue, or cross-country skiers. Whatever."

"Wait a second. You've finally managed to get to Heart's Desire and meet your literary crush, and because he's much younger and better looking than you expected, you want to leave?"

"When you put it like that, it sounds weird." My heart flutters in my chest, still on the verge of full-on panic. "I just need to get out of here ASAP. I'll explain later."

"Level with me, hun. Do you not feel safe? What aren't you telling me?"

I sniffle, shaking my head, although she can't see it. "No, it's nothing like that. He's perfectly safe, and so is his ranch. I mean, at least on a physical level—"

"Oh, I get it, " she interrupts. "Are you worried about falling in love with him?"

"Oh my gosh, Sylvia. How can you even ask me something like that? I mean, I only broke up with Olivier a couple of months ago—"

Sylvia interrupts, "You and I know that was a breakup five years in the making."

"We were only together for five years."

"That's my point. Does Chase treat you like a jerk? Act ungentlemanly or judgmental like Olivier did?"

"No."

"Does he make you feel less than? Or like he's not invested in getting to know you?"

"Not at all," I reply.

"Are you scared about the thought of his daughter?"

"Not in the least."

She whispers into the phone, though only her pugs are listening, "Is the chemistry just not there?"

Her statement couldn't be further from the truth. "No, there's definitely chemistry."

"Alright, then," she says triumphantly. "You need to get over yourself because this guy sounds perfect."

"That's the problem."

"Oh Chanel... Stubborn, stubborn, stubborn. You know, this is sooo *The Secret*."

Here comes the five-minute self-help lecture. Since Sylvia's gotten into the manifesting mindset, abundance is all I hear about. "Alright, Sylvia, tell me how this is sooo *The Secret*."

"You set your intention to visit Heart's Desire Ranch no matter what and meet Chase Heart. *That name*. Oh my gosh... And now, you're there...in a blizzard. It's perfect. Do you realize what you did, Chanel? You manifested the whole thing through tireless positive thinking and irrational faith in the outcome. It's amazing!"

"By crashing my vehicle into a snow-filled ditch? That was not me trusting my gut. That was me slamming the brakes too hard and locking my wheels on ice. The roads are treacherous here. You have no idea."

"But the universe does, and the universe wants you to be there at Heart's Desire with *gorgeous Chase* and his *adorable daughter*." She pulls the phone away, letting out a high-pitched squeal and thumping her feet excitedly on her apartment's carpeted floor. Her pugs bark excitedly to the rhythm of her feet, and I set down the phone on the bed until the commotion ceases.

She gloats, "Goodbye, stupid, sour-faced, stuck-up Olivier!"

"Tell me how you really feel about my ex," I mumble. But she's right...*about Olivier, at least.* "Aren't you listening to anything I'm saying? What's it going to take to get me out of here?"

A long pause follows, and I hear her laptop keys clicking. Swallowing loudly, she asks, "Have you seen the weather report? Meteorologists are calling this a one hundred-year storm. Short of teleportation, you're out of luck."

"I told you, I have no cell phone signal, and the internet appears to be down, too." I rub my free hand over my face. "What's the use of all the money I've made as a romance writer if I can't buy my way out of this?"

"Oh, Chanel. When are you finally going to get over your intimacy issues? Chase sounds amazing. I mean, a fellow creative whose work you know and love. There's no way I'm rescuing you. This is like something out of one of your romance novels. *Hello, horse-drawn sleigh!* What advice would you give a heroine in this situation? Turn tail and run because the guy's too cute?"

She has a point, but I'm not ready to admit it. "This is what I get for not putting on chains. The cold made me lazy. It's all my fault."

Sylvia replies with a puff of air, "Sure, you could look at it that way. But where's the magic in that?"

CHAPTER

EIGHT

CHASE

"You ready to tackle this tree?" I ask Eldon. I may have no control over what happens with Chanel, but I'm determined to make this the best Christmas possible for Maddie. Three years after my wife's death, it's time.

"Now's as good a time as any," the old man replies. I can see the gears in his head going, still sorting out what happened with Chanel and Véronique.

"After that, I better check in on the heifer," I add.

"I'm guessing tonight or tomorrow night. I'd put money on it. Smack dab in the middle of our worst storm. Fortunately, the rope's strung to the barn and the stables, so none of us can get too turned around." By rope, he means a line strung to the house we can use to find our way no matter how blinding the snow flurries fly.

Far too many stories exist of old timers who froze to death, sometimes mere feet from their front porches or barns, thanks to no visibility. Heck, legend says one of my great uncles died that way—one Heart too many in my mind.

My eyes search the great room, finding the curly-haired teen tucked in a corner with his phone and headphones. Usually, he'd hang out in the bunkhouse with the ranch hands, but I invited him to spend days at the main house for the holidays. Hollering until he finally pulls the plugs from his ears, I order, "Son, come help with the tree."

Stomping into the mudroom, we survey the shiny puddles formed around the tree, thanks to snow melt. *What a mess!* But I remind myself that this is for Maddie, and Lisa would approve.

Véronique follows behind us with her mop, swiping at our melt trail. She'll be mopping on and off all evening with how the tree's branches accumulated snow. But for our part, we did our best outside, shaking it off.

Wrestling an eight-foot tree to stand by the hearth is more than a three-person job. Still, we use a ladder, rope, and one of the ceiling beams to create enough leverage to get the behemoth seated in the heavy Christmas tree stand that's been in my family too many holiday seasons to count. The effect is breathtaking in the great room with its rich wooden floors and walls, massive granite stone hearth, and western decor.

"Wow! That's gorgeous!" Chanel's breathy voice croons behind me.

I rub my hand over my heart, too pleased by her words and unexpected presence to turn around. Suddenly, it hits me. Because of all the craziness earlier, I never properly introduced her. Making my face stony, I turn around. "Ms. Love—"

"Ms. Montgomery," she corrects, looking at me with those big, brown sugar-colored eyes that make my heart skip.

"Ms. Montgomery, allow me to formally introduce you

to everyone." Motioning towards Eldon, I say, "This here's Eldon, the ranch foreman. He's been a fixture of the place for as long as I can remember. And this is Véronique, the ranch's housekeeper and cook. She specializes in mouth-watering Basque fare. As I said before, she's ready for your cold or hot beverage requests, so please make yourself at home. And, finally, we've got Avery, who handles the stables."

I watch the blonde lean forward, taking each person's hand in turn and saying, "I'm Chanel Montgomery, but I write as Chanel Love." I admire her form-fitting turquoise turtleneck sweater and dark wash, boot-cut Ariats. She's nixed the snow boots for a pair of black cowboy boots, the pointed toes peeking from the hem of her jeans. This woman would look fine on a horse. Maybe a Palomino to match her buttery locks.

"Chanel Love?" Véronique covers her mouth with both hands to stifle the loud exclamation. But it's too late. All eyes turn to her, and her generous cheeks darken. "I've read all of your books," she confesses, rubbing her palms on her apron.

"You have?" The vivacious blonde says, a glimmer lighting her eyes. "Who's your favorite character?"

"Well, Colton, of course," the cook replies in her slight French accent, giggling. "He's *absolument parfait!*" She punctuates the declaration with a chef's kiss.

I shoot the cook a confused look.

Knitting her eyebrows, Véronique adds, "Ms. Love was one of Lisa's favorite authors, too."

The words find their mark, leaving me intrigued. Towards the end, books represented a lifeline to Lisa, distracting her from pain and fear and letting her live vicariously the life she once pursued with passion and enthusi-

51

asm. "If you wrote books that gave my wife pleasure, I'm forever grateful to you," I reply warmly.

The writer's face swims with confusion as she glances at my bare left hand.

"I'm a widower." After three years, the words still feel foreign on my tongue.

She nods, understanding flooding her face. "I'm sorry for your loss."

The room goes oppressively and awkwardly silent for a long moment.

Thankfully, Chanel breaks the tension, whispering to Véronique, "I'll sign any copies of my books you have handy."

"Oh, that would be *fantastique!*"

Clearing my throat, I grab a string of lights, plug them into the wall, and inspect them for broken bulbs. Hoping we can move past the earlier weirdness, I inquire, "So, how'd you get into writing cowboy romance anyway, California?"

She opens her arms to my daughter as she listens to my question, and the caramel-haired girl scrambles into them, hugging her tightly. God, it warms my heart to see them together.

"I'm from Truckee, but my grandparents had a ranch near Lake Tahoe. It was like a second home to me, although I would've liked it to be my first."

I open my mouth to ask another question, but Maddy beats me to it. "The tree is so beautiful, Daddy! I love it. Mama would love it, too." Halfway through the last phrase, her voice cracks, and she bursts into sobs.

Chanel embraces Maddie tightly, and the unspeakable beauty of the candid moment grips me. Clearing my throat and trying to ignore the skipping of my pulse, I explain,

"Lisa died three years ago of cancer. It wasn't on Christmas, but it was in December. So, holidays have never been the same. This is the first tree we've put up since her passing."

The blonde's eyes flood with tenderness. The kind of tenderness that could pull me into her gaze and her heart and keep me there for a long time...maybe forever. As a widower, I know that look well. It's one of the things I miss most about being married. While it terrifies one part of me, another awakens, ready to cherish it *and her.*

Her countenance and words are the healing balm I need to move past the guilt and heartache of this season. To know wholeheartedly that Lisa would bless the current situation.

But a stiff, stubborn resistance remains. Maybe it's a force of old habit. Making my voice as deep and growly as possible, I order, "Ornaments are in the boxes, but first, Eldon and I will get the lights strung. Then, I've got to get back to ranch work. It never ends, even during a blizzard."

Pursing her generous pink lips together, Chanel says in a voice as smooth and sweet as eggnog, "I'm sorry for your loss. But I'd like to do whatever I can to make this Christmas special for Maddie if that's okay with you?"

I narrow my gaze. "Why would you do that for a little girl you barely know?"

She frowns in thought. "Because I remember from my childhood—I come from a broken home—how cold and lonely Christmases felt. Like the worst time of the year instead of the best. I may not know Maddie well, but she deserves an amazing Christmas."

What's this woman doing to me? My eyes fill with tears, and I swallow hard. She's found her way into my heart, and we're less than two hours into knowing each other.

"Thank you, ma'am. That would mean a lot to me," I

manage before turning and storming towards the door. "Eldon," I call back without looking his way. "Don't try to tackle those lights alone. It's tough enough watching an old-timer like you on a saddle, let alone a ten-foot ladder. Make Avery do the climbing. I'll be back."

Hastily donning my brown Stockman Duster and white Stetson off the hook at the entrance to the mud room, I stomp the distance to the outside door, swallowed by the swirling, dark storm on the other side of the door. I don't even try to excuse my sudden departure. The bracing cold feels welcome after the warmth of the house and how that woman melted my heart inside my chest.

NINE

CHANEL

My heart throbs with recognition at the sight of Chase in the brown duster and white hat moments before he leaves the house. Even though I understand on an intellectual level that he's the author whose work I love wholeheartedly, this visual makes it real. But taking the time to process the emotions this realization brings must wait.

I'm a woman on a mission...to make a ten-year-old girl's Christmas the best possible.

"Maddie, why don't you show me which ornaments are your favorite? And if you feel up to it, you can tell me more about your mother. Talking about family members who can't be with us anymore makes them feel closer."

Véronique blinks hard, wiping her hands over her eyes. I search Maddie's face, hoping I've said the right thing. Fortunately, her expression lights up as she asks, "Who do you talk about this time of year, Chanel?"

I sigh, feeling my eyes water and my throat tighten. "My grandma and grandpa. I miss them both so much. Grandpa raised Appaloosas and American Paints and kept dairy cattle, too. Their ranch was so cozy during the holidays, kind of like this place."

"My grandparents got tired of ranching and moved to Florida when I was born, leaving everything to Daddy. It was easier when Mama was alive because he smiled back then. Kind of like he started doing again today."

My heart warms at her words, suddenly treasuring the few grins I've gotten from the grumpy cowboy.

Eldon and Avery work on the tree, stringing lights so haphazardly that I have to look away. I'm not a massive fan of heights or the way the teen defies gravity on the ten-foot ladder.

Instead, I focus on Maddie carefully unwrapping tissue-wrapped ornaments as I explain, "My mom left the family when I was a seventh-grader. It was a difficult time for my dad and me, especially after my grandparents passed. We didn't celebrate much of anything. But later, I learned that when we keep the people we love in our hearts, minds, and words—like my grandparents and your mama—they feel closer this time of year."

I hear the wind whistling as the mudroom door opens again, followed by the thud of cowboy boots. My heart soars, realizing I'm about to see Chase again. *Keep it together, Chanel. Seriously. This is about Maddie, not you or your cowboy poet.*

The little girl holds up a pale pink glass ballerina ornament, twirling and spinning to mimic it. I bite my tongue, certain it will fly from her hand and shatter on the wood floor.

To forestall the inevitable, I ask, "Maddie, what did your mama look like?"

She stops, thankfully holding the shiny trinket with

greater care. "She had beautiful long brown hair, and Daddy says I have her eyes."

I quit rustling through the box of ornaments in front of me and look at her periwinkle blues. "They're lovely, Maddie. No wonder your daddy fell in love with her."

She smiles, her eyes overflowing with warmth. "She always gave the best kisses and hugs, and I miss her bedtime stories. Daddy doesn't have time to read to me at night."

"Maybe I could...before you go to bed. Unless that's something you want to keep between you and your mama?"

The little girl's face beams. "I would love to have you read to me! Will it be one of your books?"

Aware someone's watching me, I look up. Chase leans against the wall on the other side of the massive great room. His eyes are red-rimmed, and he doesn't try to hide it. He intently watches my conversation with his daughter, his hands shoved in his jeans pockets and one leg bent with the sole of his boot resting against the wall.

My cheeks warm under his tempestuous gaze. "Well, my books are romances for grown-up people. You know, like Hallmark Christmas movies."

She shrugs. "Sometimes Véronique watches those. But they're kind of boring to me, with all that kissing stuff.'"

I raise my head, catching Chase's golden-green eyes, ready to make a joke about enjoying this precious time while Maddie still thinks boys have the cooties. Instead, his searing gaze sets my heart aflame and lodges a knot in my throat. Why I thought it would be safe to capture this man's attention on the subject of kissing, I don't know.

Clearing my throat, I tell Maddie, "Maybe we could

settle for something on your bookshelves. Do you have any Christmas reads?"

She stops, dropping the ornaments in her hands on the couch and clapping loudly. "I have *'Twas the Night Before Christmas*. Would you read that to me?" Her plump cheeks glow, and her eyes light up, warming my heart.

"It's a date, then. But before we can even think about bedtime and reading, we've got a massive tree to decorate. And maybe some cookies to make?" I look questioningly towards Véronique.

The French woman smiles politely. "How about I get started on some gingerbread people? That way, you can take shifts, decorating cookies and the tree. Oh, and who can I bring eggnog or other refreshments to?"

"I would love some eggnog," I reply.

"Me, too!" Maddie says.

"Ms. Montgomery, would you like the adult or kid version?"

"The adult version, thank you. And please call me Chanel."

The cook nods. Her eyebrows raise as her head bobbles back and forth between the two cowboys.

Chase clears his throat, answering gruffly, "We're sticking to black coffee tonight. In case that heifer gives birth."

The ever-curious writer in me comes out. "Is it normal for calves to be born in December?"

"No, ma'am, but we had an incident with a bull that escaped its enclosure six months ago. I think you can figure out the rest."

"And you think the calf will be born tonight? Will it survive being born out of season?"

He shrugs. "As long as it's healthy, and we keep an extra eye on it, the calf should be fine."

Not sure whether I'll regret the next question, I ask anyway. "Would you mind if I help out tonight...watching the cow and baby or whatever it is you do? It'd be great research for one of my books."

"In that case, go light on the eggnog. "

"Should I stick to black coffee like you two?"

His unreadable face breaks into a grin, warm and stunning. I notice his smiles keep increasing in frequency the longer we talk. "I'm joking. The cow does all the hard work. We stand by and step in as needed. As long as you can see straight, you'll be fine."

"I'm not going for tipsy, just cozy. Besides, I've got a date with Maddie for a bedtime story, so I need to be in top form."

"Thank you," Chase says from a place so deep in his heart that it puts warmth in his voice and eyes, infusing the space between us with a quiet intimacy. "Véronique has been a huge help with Maddie, providing the female touch she needs over the years. But she's usually home this time of night, and I have too much on my plate for bedtime story reading, even though your conversation today made it clear I've underestimated how much it means to Maddie. Véronique, why don't you put some Christmas music on."

Soon, country Christmas carols fill the air. Dolly Parton. Randy Travis. The Judds. Kenny Rogers. Reba McEntire.

Maddie, Eldon, Avery, Chase, and I decorate the tree. In the kitchen, the sounds of banging pots and a mixer give way to delicious fragrances—ginger, cloves, molasses, cinnamon. My holidays have never felt cozier, basking in the light and warmth of this gorgeous, rough-hewn mountain ranch.

"Smells like we're going to have cookies to decorate and taste soon." I smile down at Maddie.

The little girl jumps, twirling around. "I'm having so much fun with you, Chanel. How are you going to decorate your gingerbread people?"

I purse my lips, thinking. "Well, I need at least one Elsa cookie. And there's got to be another like Gingy from *Shrek*."

The little girl laughs, her golden burnished curls dancing atop her shoulders. "And you need a cowboy," she adds.

"Of course," I agree with a wink.

My eyes wander to the tender gaze of the man hanging ornaments next to me. The corners of Chase's mouth remain turned up ever so slightly, leaving me desperate to know what he's thinking. And I imagine my ear-to-ear grin creates plenty of curiosity on his end, too.

TEN

After a scrumptious dinner of hearty beef stew and freshly baked rosemary and olive oil bread, Maddie and I dive into a marathon of holiday fun. We frost so many cookies that I'm sure my fingers will remain sticky for days. We hang so many ornaments my arms ache, and we fill our heads with enough carols for fifty Christmases.

The cowboy poet saunters into the kitchen, the rugged sound of leather-tooled boots on wood flooring announcing his arrival. He's done this on and off all night, stealing cookies here and there and acting as the unofficial taste tester. He's even decorated a few—all grumpy-faced cowboys.

Chase is a sight to behold, and even though I've spent the whole night drinking him in with my eyes, I can't tear them away now. I've read his book so many times over the past few months that snippets of his poetry keep coming to me as I look at him.

Relegating the profoundness of those words and images with the hunk before me is no easy matter. On top of that, reading his work makes me feel a one-sided intimacy, like I've been inside his mind.

Sylvia is right. I need to see this through, whatever's going on. I can't let fear of rejection and loss hold me back, especially when everything about him is so wonderful, from his attentiveness to me to the easy affection he shares with his adoring daughter.

"What do you think of our masterpieces, Daddy?" The girl squeals, reaching up to hug him. It's the first time I've been jealous of my adolescent Christmas helper since meeting her.

No one hugs in my family, which left me affection-starved as a kid. It didn't help in adulthood when I gravitated towards hands-off guys like Olivier. I guess because those men didn't trigger my fear of intimacy. But what I wouldn't give to open my arms and get scooped up by Chase's strength and warmth now. My cheeks burn at the thought as he eyes me with a dimpled, lop-sided grin, his short, thick chestnut hair curling at the ends.

"They're beautiful, baby girl. Absolutely festive."

"You have to eat one," she challenges.

"I've already eaten so many I may not get my belt buckled tomorrow." He laughs deep in his throat, rubbing the flat abs beneath his button-down flannel. His voice has a newfound tenderness I thirst to hear more of.

How my grump has gone from gruff to a golden retriever boggles my mind. What boggles it even more is the use of "my" in his context. I guess it's wishful thinking inspired by a night of thick tension and unending eye contact.

"You have to eat one more!" she orders. "And one of Chanel's, too."

The cowboy eyes the spread of green, white, blue, and

red gingerbread people with practiced amazement, pointing out his favorites. Finally, he grabs a messy one bearing the bravado of a ten-year-old artist, downing it in one ferocious, grizzly-sized gulp.

Maddie shakes her head, belly laughing until Chase and I join her. His eyes meet mine again, and my heart does another dizzy twirl. This will never get old. Then, he winks, sending my pulse racing faster than the Polar Express.

"Alright, California, I can handle one more. But only one. Which of these will it be?" he points towards my artfully decorated, tidy rows, taking them in one at a time until his finger settles on a blue and white one with yellow hair and pink cheeks and lips. "Ah, Elsa, the Ice Princess. How about we get rid of her?"

I nod, feeling dangerously close to tears. I don't know what it is about tonight that has me so emotional. The cowboy grabs the cookie, feigning a second attempt at gobbling it to make his daughter laugh some more. Only this time, he savors it instead, taking one careful bite after the next as his eyes twinkle, fixed on mine.

Finishing, he exclaims, "I just figured it out."

"Figured what out?"

"Your new nickname."

I shrug, fighting a smile. "New nickname?"

"Goldie."

"Like Goldie Hawn?"

"No, like Golden State, since the California endearment doesn't quite fit you. Golden blonde," he continues, drawing close enough to wrap the end of a lock of my hair possessively around his pointer finger, stroking it with his thumb. I've never felt more jealous of hair in my life. "And the mineral...you know, the stuff men risk their lives, wealth, and sanity for a chance at?" He arches his eyebrow, continuing to stare unabashedly.

I swallow hard, desperate to control my breathing and heart rate, but a breathy sigh still escapes my lips. My cheeks burn brighter than Rudolph's nose. Judging by the satisfied look on his face and the sparks zinging from his eyes to mine, none of these details are lost on him.

Thoroughly exacerbated by my body's mutiny, I go for the only thing left to me—a mostly steady voice. "If I didn't know better, I'd say you got some of that adult eggnog."

He scowls, suddenly channeling a delicious desperado vibe. "Nope, sober as a church mouse." Narrowing his gaze and drawing closer to me, he confesses, "But there are ways to get punch-drunk that have nothing to do with alcohol, Goldie. Like spending the evening staring at true beauty... That said, you have yet to give your opinion. What do you think of my new nickname? It has to be better than ice princess..."

"I get the impression you'd like to see her go away."

"Or, she could...you know, invite the prince into her castle. Quit being so lonely. Let that snowy heart of hers do a little melting. What do you think?"

My hand reflexively goes to my chest, and I swallow hard. The sparks in his eyes transform into flames, letting me know we left Disney behind a while ago. "That would require the right prince...or cowboy."

"Good," he says with a confident nod as Maddie rubs her eyes, looking utterly exhausted. He ruffles his daughter's hair. "Alright, we've kept our guest up long enough. Off to bed, little one. Véronique'll get you ready, and then Chanel will be up to read to you."

Turning to me, the cowboy nods towards the great room. "Come have one more look at the tree with me."

"Okay," I reply, savoring the sparks zinging back and forth between us.

The lights of the great room glow at their lowest setting, casting the expanse in an intimate glow enhanced by the roaring fire and glittering tree. "This place is beautiful, Chase. I can't wrap my head around how cozy it feels. Like the perfect Christmas."

"I've spent forty-two Christmases in this room, which lets me safely attest that what makes this one so beautiful is you, Chanel."

My heart pitter-patters as my eyes wander to his very kissable lips. The ends of his mouth turn up, and he leans forward, closing the distance between us. Suddenly, a strange swooshing comes within inches of our heads, making me jump and swat at my hair.

"What in the—" exclaims the cowboy, craning his neck.

A rustle of feathers breaks the silence. "Is that a bat or a bird?" By the end of the sentence, my voice climbs an octave as I reflexively turn to Chase, burying my head against his hard chest with my eyes squeezed shut. "Please make it go away." My voice trembles as the unreasonable request tumbles from my mouth.

A deep rumble of laughter bubbles up from his chest, sending low, delicious vibrations through me. "It's an owl. Are you afraid of them?"

"I'm afraid of anything that lands in hair."

"That's kind of an odd phobia," Chase replies, wrapping his arms around me. He settles his chin atop my head, filling me with warmth and strength despite the bird of prey on the loose.

I glance up into his face. "Not when you have light blonde hair. Everything's attracted to the color—bats, hummingbirds, butterflies, hornets..."

Another fly-by close enough to hear confirms the statement. Chase walks me backward out of the great room until we stand in the entrance to the kitchen. His big hands find their way into my hair, and he strokes my tresses, gently massaging the base of my skull and neck. The gesture instantly soothes me, despite the feathered friend flying nearby. I melt into his arms, and he lets out a long, satisfied sigh.

"I'd be lying if I said your pretty locks didn't attract me, too," he drawls, fixing on my eyes as his face grows serious.

Searching the area for the owl again, my eyes shoot to the ceiling directly above us. His follow, our gazes resting on the same green sprig with white berries and a red bow.

"Mistletoe," we say simultaneously, laughing at the synchronicity.

Clearing his throat, Chase says, "I wonder who put that up there, although my guess is Véronique. She's always trying to get a smooch out of poor Eldon."

"Does he not return her feelings?" I ask, savoring the spicy, woodsy smell of his cologne.

"He's a lifelong bachelor, so he's unsure of what to do." Our eyes lock, and he adds, "I just need one more minute, Mr. Owl." Dimples dent his cheeks as he dips his head, letting his soft, warm lips graze tenderly over mine. Every point of contact lights a spark until my skin glows, incandescent. My right hand comes up to his sculpted shoulder, and he grabs it with his left, pressing it firmly over his chest where his heart booms.

Shivers of pleasure travel up and down the back of my head and into my neck, where his other hand remains tangled in my hair. His breath warms my cheek as he changes the angle of his head, deepening the kiss. My lips part on a sigh, and he claims me with increasing urgency, his tongue exploring my mouth with a gentle authority that leaves my brain light-headed and my heart dancing.

Another whoosh races past my shoulders and back, and I pull away reluctantly. "I'm sorry, but I can't take any more of your nighttime visitor."

He chuckles. "Must've come in with the tree. I imagine he's far more scared than you or me. But let me walk you upstairs to Maddie's room."

"Will you stay with me until I'm done reading? So, you can accompany me to the guest bedroom and protect me from the flying menace?"

"Of course," he replies, grabbing my hand and leisurely strolling across the great room. "I won't let that old bird touch one lock on your pretty head."

CHAPTER

ELEVEN

CHANEL

Maddie's voice sounds more like a sleepwalker than an awake little girl as she drawls, "Please read to me, Chanel. Like you promised, and whatever you do, don't leave without saying goodbye. You have to promise me."

Her words make me tear up, and Chase's eyes look red, too, a muscle jumping in his jaw. I hug the little girl, kissing her petal-soft cheek, already warm with sleep, and reassuring her, "I'll be here in the morning for Christmas Day. But you have to sleep fast so Santa will come."

She's out when her head hits the pillow, but I still read to her for a few minutes to keep my promise. Chase's gentle eyes never leave my face, and I feel gloriously, dangerously close to falling for him...*hard*. Honestly, I already have.

When I close the book and set it on the bookshelf, he smiles, nodding towards the door. We head into the hallway, quietly closing the door to her room behind us.

He shoves his hands in his jeans pockets as he escorts me down the hallway to the guest bedroom, whispering,

"Maddie didn't get to say goodbye when Lisa passed. This whole thing has been so tough on her."

"And you, too," I add, looking into his warm, sad face.

He nods, looking away to study the floor's grains as he collects himself. We stand before the guest bedroom door, but I don't want to say goodnight.

Suddenly, his teary gaze captures mine. "I'd like to invite you back downstairs to help with presents and Maddie's stocking. But there's the owl…" He frowns.

I hesitate for one moment, steeling my nerves. "Maybe if we turn on the room lights, he'll stop flying everywhere. Or at least I'll see him coming. What do you think?"

He shrugs, grinning. "I'm not an owl whisperer or anything, but we can give it a try."

The blizzard howls outside, massive gusts of wind shaking the house from the floorboards to the rafters. Downstairs, Chase turns up the lights as Eldon, Véronique, and Avery appear, gorgeous pre-wrapped packages in their hands that they place under the large tree.

Staring at the presents, I say, "But I thought you didn't celebrate Christmas. Where did the gifts come from?"

The man shrugs. "I've always made sure Maddie has presents, and she also gets them from her grandparents and aunts and uncles on her mom's side. But the tree and decorations? That's been a long time coming."

Eldon grumbles, "What's the deal with the bright lights?"

Chase laughs. "Would you believe there's an owl in here? He keeps swooping down on us. Chanel figured the lights might help him know his place."

The ranch foreman shrugs. "Good, maybe he can take care of the family of mice that scurried out of the tree earlier."

I cover my mouth, my eyes darting around the room. "If I see a mouse, so help me, Chase, you'll have to carry me up the stairs."

The cowboy laughs affably, wrapping an arm around my waist protectively. "It's a deal. I won't let anything happen to you, Goldie. You're safe with me."

And I do feel safe and warm and loved in this man's presence. Like no one's ever made me feel before.

Avery chimes in, "Maddie and I saw them scurry out of the tree earlier when you guys were busy turning Eldon into Heart Desire's poet laureate."

"How do you know what a poet laureate is?" Chase asks, taken aback.

The teen shrugs, looking down. "English is my best subject."

"Welcome to the club." I smile, glancing at the handsome cowboy poet.

"Speak for yourself, Goldie. Science and geology were my best subjects."

"In the context of your poems and drawings, that doesn't surprise me."

Rubbing his neck, he grins. "I'd like to discuss what you think of my work later. Now that you're over your Eldon infatuation."

The old man grumbles, and the cook frowns.

I shake my head, and Chase chuckles, tangling his fingers with mine and leading me to the hearth. We hang Maddie's stocking on the mantle, filling it with small toys, oranges, and candies.

On the hearth, we offer Santa a plate of gingerbread cookies and a glass of milk. Eldon takes a single bite from one of the sweets, leaving Maddie's Christmas letter nearby. At the top of her wishlist, I read, "Make Daddy smile again."

Hot tears streak down my cheeks, and I try to wipe them away discreetly. But Chase catches me. Palming my face, he uses his thumbs to finish the job, beaming at me. "That's one Christmas wish answered, thanks to you." Warmth spills over from his eyes into my heart, and I never want this magical night to end.

But, eventually, laughing turns to yawning, and Chase escorts me politely up the stairs to the guest room. He wishes me goodnight at the door with a long, tender kiss. Wrapped tightly in his firm, strong arms, I have the strange impression I'm finally home. It simultaneously scares and thrills me.

"Thank you for everything you did to bring joy to Maddie tonight...and to me, too," he whispers, reluctantly letting me go and turning towards the stairs. Halfway to the banister, he looks over his shoulder, catching me staring after him. Turning to face me again, he flashes the first ear-to-ear grin I've ever seen light up his face. In a loud whisper, he says, "I forgot to ask you what you want for Christmas, Goldie."

I giggle, looking down for a moment in thought. For the owl and mice to go back outside? Certainly, but that's too boring. More cookies and eggnog? That's a foregone conclusion.

Finally, it hits me. "Two things."

He looks surprised. "Okay..."

"I'd like to see the calf when the time's right."

"Of course. And?"

"And I'd like my favorite author and artist to sign my copy of his book."

Pleasure lights up his handsome face, and his Adam's Apple bobs as he swallows hard. "Done and done."

"But you haven't told me what you want for Christmas yet?"

His adorable dimples deepen, and his straight white teeth flash. Sounding breathless, he confesses, "Honestly, I'd like some more time with you under the mistletoe. You make me feel amazing, Goldie. Better than I thought I'd ever feel again. Would that be okay?"

My voice catches in my throat. "More than okay."

"Good. Now, shut that door before the owl comes hunting for you." With a confident wink, he turns, descending the stairs.

I lean on the other side of the closed door, breathing hard. Is this what being bowled over feels like? My heart performs a percussion solo. My breathing feels like I just summited Everest. Pure, exhilarating joy courses through my veins and arteries.

I can't stop smiling through my shower and nighttime routine. After changing into my pajamas, I sink into the welcoming bed, my fingertips tracing my lips as my mind runs through the cowboy's sizzling kisses again and again.

I AWAKEN to the spooky sound of an owl's call from the great room. It echoes off the wood and stone, amplifying and reverberating as it reaches my bedroom. I lie in my soft blue and green flannel pajamas and fluffy robe atop the quilts of the bed. I must've fallen asleep. Now, though, I'm wide awake, unable to shut the sound of the offending bird out of my head.

Replaying the incredible evening with Chase, Maddie,

and everyone, my heart feels full to bursting, and it glows with a newfound warmth and intensity I'm not used to. Suddenly, I burst into tears, a thousand new fears following the pleasurable remembrances.

What if this doesn't last? What if Chase ever leaves me? What if something happens to Maddie? My head swirls with anxious thoughts, all centering around loss and abandonment.

I know where this comes from—my mother's departure. It was the first time I realized people we love desperately, who we rely on for our happiness and very existences, can leave in a flash. Without warning and never to return.

Wide awake and unable to sleep, I grab the cordless phone on the nightstand beside my bed. The alarm clock reads ten thirty. Fortunately, Sylvia's a dedicated late-night person. She's likely not even on her second wind yet.

She answers on the third ring. "I thought you were never going to call. Girl, you left me on a cliffhanger. What's going on with gorgeous Chase?"

I take a deep breath. "Sylvia, you were right. The universe did bring me here, and now I know why…"

She waits.

My tongue darts out to wet my lips.

"Oh, come on, you can't leave me hanging like this… Spit it out."

"I know this will sound completely insane, rash, stupid, the whole nine yards. But I wouldn't say it if I didn't believe it with every ounce of my soul…"

"What?" she screams into the phone.

I burst into sobs, swiping tears with my free hand.

"What happened? Are you okay? Tell me what's going on?"

On a shuddering exhale, the words rush from me in a

torrent. "I'm in love with gorgeous Chase. And I'm not talking about crushing hard or gobsmacked or in lust or any of those things. I'm talking totally enamored, can't look at anybody else in the room, blood on fire kind of in love with him. And he's acting the same way about me."

She must pull the phone away from her face because her voice sounds distant as she squeals. It sends her two grouchy pugs into a barking frenzy. Over the pooch chaos, she yells, "Oh my goodness! You mean, like Eliza and Colton in love?" She's referring to my first bestseller, *Love's Promise.*

"Worse than that," I say, still cradling my head and trying not to hyperventilate. "Like ready for a panic attack, afraid I'm someday going to lose him, terrified in love."

"Honey..." she croons, accompanied by a doggy choir in the background. "Hold on a second." The barking gets fuzzy, like she's muting the receiver on her leg. "Quiet down, you little punks!"

It takes a few minutes for the dogs to silence and for her to return to the line. During said minutes, I go from hyperventilating back to sobbing.

"Oh, Chanel..."

"What am I going to do?" I struggle through sobs. "I've never felt this way about anybody before."

"But you said he feels the same way. So, isn't that a good thing?"

I take a deep, shuddering breath, "I think he does, and yes, that's a very good thing. But he's got a ten-year-old daughter, and I'm in love with her, too, which means in under ten hours, my entire heart's been taken over by two people I will never be able to survive losing. And it scares the heck out of me."

She pauses for a long moment. "It's only natural to feel

this way. You have abandonment issues, thanks to your mom and how everything went down with your dad and Georgia."

"That's another thing... What if I end up hurting Maddie someday? What if I become like Georgia, and she hates me?"

Sylvia's voice sounds more firm as she counters, "Okay, first of all, that would never happen because you're nothing like Georgia. Just like you're nothing like your bio mom. You are a loving, funny, talented, amazing human being, and any man and children who share their lives with you will be truly lucky."

"Thank you," I sniffle, wiping the tears from my cheeks. "But how do I deal with this feeling like I could someday lose them?"

She replies, "We all have those fears. But if you let them get the better of you, you'll lose Chase and Maddie for sure. From what you've told me, they're worth taking a chance on, no matter what the future holds. After all, love is a gamble for everyone involved. But it's a gamble worth taking."

Her words both comfort and shame me. How can I be the one freaking out about loss after everything Chase and Maddie have endured?

I whisper. "You always say exactly what I need to hear."

"That's what friends are for, and you do the same for me whenever I need it."

I clear my throat, hesitant to voice the thought weighing on my mind. But I have to. If anyone would know the answer, it's Sylvia. "If people can manifest good things in their life, and you believe I somehow attracted Chase and Maddie into mine, what about the bad stuff? Like Chase's first wife, Lisa, dying so young? Or my mom abandoning

Dad and me? Why does bad stuff happen? I mean, surely no one intentionally manifests that kind of pain."

She replies softly, "I don't think we'll ever have the answers to those questions, at least in this existence. But since there is bad in the world, it's even more important to rejoice and hold onto the good. Gratefulness beats out fear every time. And living in the present is an antidote to anxiety. So, savor every moment getting to know gorgeous Chase and his adorable daughter, and never, ever take anything for granted."

"You're right," I sniffle.

"Oh, honey, I am so, so happy for you. Nobody deserves this more than you. I wish I was there to hug you!"

"Me, too. Merry Christmas, by the way!"

"Merry Christmas to you, too! And pug hugs from sunny California!"

CHAPTER

TWELVE

CHASE

T hree o'clock in the morning rolls around, and I should trudge out of the warm barn, through the whistling snow-laden wind, and back towards the house guided by the rope. It's Eldon's turn to take a shift with the heifer. She has yet to give birth, and I have yet to notice telltale signs she's close, like stretching or looking back at her abdomen.

In truth, I may not even need to be out here. In all likelihood, mom and baby will do fine without me. Nine times out of ten, nature handles things. The most I can probably offer is a good start with colostrum and a quick calf dry-off and warm-up, which this toasty barn already has semi-handled.

Yet, I remain glued to the cot where I sit, three-quarters of the way through Chanel's book, *Love's Promise*, and crying like a baby. I asked Véronique if I could borrow it earlier. Apparently, she keeps a small stash of romance books behind the cookbooks in the kitchen. The copy she gave me has "Lisa Heart" written in neat, frail print on the inside title page. The handwriting confirms the nudge the universe has been giving me all night to read Chanel's book.

But Véronique neglected to tell me it's the story of a widower learning to love again—the figurative Sheriff Colton. And I jumped right in without reading the description on the back or the reviews, not wanting anything to taint my first impression of her work.

I've wept over countless passages, marveling at Chanel's depth and breadth of understanding of grief in its many forms. Her ability to describe the pain of loss, her words of comfort to the survivors who have to go on even when they feel more dead than alive. Who'd have thought such comfort would come from a pink five-by-eight tome covered in wildflowers?

Colton's wife, Clementine, dies in childbirth, leaving him to raise their baby daughter alone. He relies on milk from the family cow and the kind advice of female neighbors, trying not to bond too closely with the infant— refusing to name her and assuming she will die, too. But only when he finally starts loving the baby wholeheartedly, naming her Lily, does she thrive. Eventually, Colton notices the schoolmarm, Eliza, who's sworn off love but can't keep her eyes off him. A heartfelt, passionate romance blossoms as they realize they must surrender to love to find the family both crave.

Some passages remind me of the great room earlier when my gaze remained glued on my pretty houseguest as she celebrated the holiday with Maddie. It's been a long time since a sight stole my heart and breath so wholly.

The book fortifies something I've lived long enough to realize. Some things you know—deep in your bones and with every cell in your body. You may be unable to quantify or explain them, but that doesn't make them any less real or right. And that's the only way I can describe my growing conviction that I *need* Chanel Montgomery—not for one day, or one night, or one year, but for as many days and nights and years as I can fathom hitching a ride on this rotating blue and green globe.

The way she looked at me tonight, the fire kindled by our mistletoe kisses. I can tell she feels it, too. Precious emotions, the kind you don't squander or ignore.

But then, this book happened... Looking at the copyright, I see she published it four years ago, yet it speaks to me in ways nothing has since Lisa's departure. Reading one poignantly worded passage after the next that articulates the haunting swirl of emotions I've felt over the last few years heals me in ways I can't explain or express...but that I've needed without even realizing it.

The places in my heart where scars once riveted the flesh into a hard, cold, immovable structure suddenly feel softened, warmed, made flexible once more. The scars don't go away. They never will. But they take on a new form, somehow strengthening me, reinforcing my resilience, preparing me for the crazy, wild recklessness of falling head over heels, madly in love with Chanel.

Rooting for Colton to take a second chance on love with Eliza, for himself and his daughter's sake, makes me feel a little more okay with the unexpected events of the last twelve hours.

Still, something holds me back, nags at my conscience, as if I need permission one more time from my beloved wife, Lisa. To my shock and surprise, I find it on page three hundred and twenty-seven of Chanel's novel as an underlined passage with hearts drawn in the margin and my name.

It reads, "It suddenly made sense to me—what people

had been trying to tell me for all these months. Making room in my heart and life for Eliza didn't mean excising Clementine from it. My first wife would always be a part of me, the best part of me. But so would Eliza, and these two things didn't have to be mutually exclusive because love is forever in its abundance. There's always more than enough, more than we can possibly fathom, and the more we allow our hearts to feel and absorb it, the more love we put back into the world."

My fingers trace the ink of my wife's pen as tears pour down my cheeks, wetting my beard, and I place one last kiss on the page. "Thank you, my love," I say to the ether— whatever and whoever's listening. There's a finality to it, no longer tragic but bittersweet, and I swear even the sound of the storming wind dies away momentarily, lulled by the magic of the sacred moment.

How could Lisa be so strong and loving, so selfless and generous in her last days, providing this intimate message for me when I need it most? Left to me in a book penned by the woman who feels increasingly like my future? As if both somehow had a hand in writing my past and future—an otherworldly, timeless sort of agreement.

And how could God, in His boundless generosity, make time for this quiet moment and this revelation? After I spent three years with my heart hardened against Him, furious for taking my wife?

The only answer to these questions remains *love*.

The heifer bedded nearby shifts, letting me know things are finally progressing. Stretching follows, and a couple of long looks at her belly. She even kicks at it a few times.

Chanel might be angry at me for sparing her the more graphic parts of mammal birth, but I've got to pull myself together. And I've got to finish her book so when I see the sunshiny literati again, I can say with the same certainty that she does to me that I've read her work, and I'm her biggest fan.

The kind of fan who wants to do more than stand in line at book signings for her autograph. The kind of fan who needs to snuggle her close every night, keeping her safe, loved, and adored for as long as I draw breath.

The heifer stomps her back foot, and I set down the book, running my hands over my tear-streaked face. I may not have every answer regarding how, when, and why things will work out with Chanel. But deep down in my gut, I know they will.

The proof is in the serendipity that brought me and Chanel Montgomery to this moment in the first place. The interstellar magic, or whatever you want to call it, that placed us on the same sphere at the same time in the same vicinity. And all of it despite my bitter stubbornness when it came to meeting her.

A thousand concentric circles converged to bring this one breathtaking chance into being—the storm of a century, a four-year-old bestselling novel, a three-year-old message, misuse of car brakes, a haphazardly gathered Christmas tree, a heifer calving at the wrong time, a stash of books only the housekeeper knew about, a little girl hungry for Christmas festivities. The list goes on and on...

The cow bellows, declaring it's time to put all thoughts aside except those related to ranching and cattle.

In my gentlest voice, I encourage, "You're alright, Mama, and you'll have a new baby to show for it soon."

There's something remarkably fitting about this warm barn in the dead of winter. Looking at my watch, I realize the date's significance—December twenty-fifth. Christmas morning, sitting in a modern-day manger, welcoming new life.

THIRTEEN

CHASE

I awaken with a startle, listening to the low, nurturing grunts of a mother cow to her bleating calf. Rubbing my hands over my face to the scratchy sound of my beard, I realize I somehow managed to fall asleep after the birth.

Chanel's book lies next to me, opened on the last page, and though I've hardly had enough sleep to cover the night, my heart bursts with expectation at the thought of seeing my Goldie again. Pulling back the curtain behind the makeshift cot, I peer into a world of infinite white. Storm of the century it is.

Stretching, the strains and pains of my body let me know cowboy cots no longer cut it. Lord only knows how poor Eldon feels after spending a night out here. Heading into the bare-bones bathroom, I survey myself in the dim, scratched mirror. Brushing my teeth and washing my face and neck with bracing cold water from the tap, I smell the rich minerals of Colorado's red earth.

Combing my mahogany waves, I grab the scissors on the sink, trimming my facial hair until I resemble something halfway neat and clean. I need a hot shower and a change of clothes, though. No doubt, I smell like the barn.

My watch reads seven-thirty. Enough time to pull myself together before bringing Chanel out here to see the calf.

I feel guilty about not getting her out here sooner, but large mammal live births can be a little traumatizing the first time around. I'd prefer starting with more pleasant ranch experiences, like collecting hen's eggs, giving treats to ornery goats, or combing the horses. Besides, I need the time to clean up after Mama and baby and get my heart and mind prepared for what comes next—figuring out how to keep the romance writer destiny crashed into my driveway ditch.

Inside, I steal coffee from the pot, winking at Véronique. She puts the Chanel Love romance novel in her hand down guiltily, but I smile. "Tough not to have the reading bug with the author in our home."

She smiles, raising her eyebrow curiously.

"Thank you for the loan of the book last night. I'd like to say I'll return it to your stash. But I feel greedy with Ms. Montgomery's words and want to cherish them for myself. I promise I'll buy you another copy."

"Well, of course," she replies, blushing. "After all, it was Lisa's book."

I nod, leaning down to hug the plump cook. "If I haven't said it recently, thank you for all you've done over the past few years to help me through things. I couldn't have done it without you."

Her eyebrows fly away as countless questions land on her face, but I have plenty to do before I see Chanel again. And before we celebrate Christmas together for the first time. "Now, if you'll excuse me, I'm heading upstairs for a much-needed shower."

On the way up, I pause in the great room, taking in the festive wonder of the sparkling tree, heavy-laden with ornaments. Some have passed down through my family for so long they're older than me. Beneath the branches, piles of red, green, and gold packages gleam, decorated with artful bows.

From the second-story interior balcony, I search the rafters, finding the owl perched near the top of the roof's peak. Even if I could capture it, I wouldn't have the heart to put it outside in this weather. When we do manage to get a hold of the bird, though, the barn will be an ideal spot for relocation. Chanel may feel a little nervous about the whole thing, but I plan on keeping her safe and close.

Hot streams of water in the shower soothe the ache of my cot-weary muscles, reinvigorating me. A fresh red and black flannel shirt and Wranglers continue the transformation from a tired rancher to a man with enough room in his heart for holiday cheer...*at last*. Despite the lack of sleep, I feel like a live wire, bursting with energy. Soon, the smell of pancakes, eggs, and bacon siren calls me to the top of the stairs, and I hear joyful voices on the first floor.

My heart beats out of my chest as I stroll into the kitchen, stopping in the archway to the great room as Chanel turns to face me, her cheeks glowing. *More time under the mistletoe, indeed...*

Suddenly, all eyes are on us, and Eldon breaks the silence. "Time to cowboy up, Buster."

"Well, I guess it is," I say with a lopsided grin, captivated by the writer's lovely face and alluring form in a soft pale pink cashmere sweater and light wash skinny jeans with brown ankle booties.

The blonde's ear-to-ear grin welcomes me, and my pulse pounds in my temples. Pulling her slowly into my arms, I savor the feel of her petite body, as if God hand-carved her to rest right next to my heart.

"Did you sleep well?" I ask, leaning in to taste her juicy pink lips. She stands on her tiptoes, wrapping her arms around my neck and enthusiastically returning the embrace. Leaning back to capture my eyes with her gaze, she says, "The owl woke me up a couple of times."

"Really?" I say, capturing her mouth again and enjoying the heady shivers that travel from my lips to my heart, making it boom against my ribs. She nods, her lips still pressed to mine, and I lift her off the ground, gently twirling her around until everyone laughs.

Eldon hollers, "Alright, you two, quit hogging that plant." He jumps up, headed our direction.

But I'm sure as heck not about to let the old-timer have a go at my woman. Wrapping my arm around Chanel's slim waist, I maneuver us out from under the verdant sprig, challenging the ranch hand. "Why don't you and Véronique give it a whirl?"

The ranch foreman blusters, but the cook covers the distance before he can say much. Her eyes twinkle as he finally gives in, planting one on her, his extravagant handlebar mustache leading the way. She laughs, blushing to the collar of her blouse. The old ranch hand looks down timidly, his face aglow as he reaches for her hand, clasping it warmly. *Yep, he's a goner.*

Maddie laughs, clapping her hands together, and Avery gives his best unimpressed eighteen-year-old face.

Grabbing Chanel's hand, I call over my shoulder. "We'll be back for some grub and presents, but it's time for me to keep my promise to our writer-in-residence and show her the newest arrival."

Behind me, Maddie exclaims, "A new baby! I want to see!"

Véronique's wise voice chimes in, "You have breakfast to finish first. Your daddy will take you to see the baby when it's time." I don't want to exclude my daughter from the unveiling. But growing up on a ranch, she's seen more than her fair share of calves and baby animals, and I need some alone time with our guest.

I lead Chanel to the mudroom door, stopping to help her into her leather coat, cap, and mittens before we head outside, trudging through the white-washed swirl of the unceasing blizzard, hanging onto the rope like a lifeline.

Once inside, my heart fills to bursting as I watch the slim blonde run forward towards the mom and baby, covering her mouth with a scarlet mitten and cooing in delight.

Covering the distance between us, I wrap my arms around her from behind, snuggling her against my body and burying my head in the warm spot at the crook of her neck where soft waves of gold gather. She melts into my embrace, sighing as she covers my glove with her own.

"This feels so good," she says breathlessly. "Too good. Like, how can we make it last good?" I hear a shakiness in her voice, as if she's on the verge of crying.

Squeezing her more tightly, I whisper. "One day at a time for the rest of our lives." Closing my eyes, I savor her vanilla-cinnamon smell, fighting the tears that fill my eyes. Holding her like this feels like coming home. A lump lodges in my throat as I realize despite thinking I'd never love again, I could make a life with this woman.

Clearing my throat, I say, "You know that rope strung between the house and the barn that we used to find our way through the storm? That's what you've been for me this Christmas. Helping me find my way back to happiness and joy that I thought I'd never feel again. Especially after the soul-numbing blizzard that engulfed me with Lisa's death. I know you may have to leave...that you have a home to return to...eventually. But I can't let you go without telling you how much this Christmas means to me...means to all of us. Or how much I need you in my life. We all do, Goldie."

She sobs quietly, clinging to my hands. I wait patiently, infusing her with my warmth and love until she feels ready to speak. "I was twelve when Mom abandoned our family, leaving my dad for her high school sweetheart, a man she reconnected with over the internet. Unfortunately, she was never especially good at multi-tasking, so when she reforged the old connection, she burned all her new ones, leaving the family she claimed to love behind..."

She pauses, sniffling and drawing a deep breath. I hold her more tightly, feeling my heart boom against her back. "The worst part was trying to figure out what I could have done differently to make her love us more. To make her stay...certain it was somehow my fault. I wanted her to return, even more than for myself, for my dad, who never recovered, walking around for years with a hole in his heart. Eventually, he remarried a woman, who I can only describe as a narcissist, Georgia. She made my life miserable and ensured I felt unwelcome, no matter how cheerful and kind I tried to be. I guess, because of all of that, I've always been afraid of *this*..." She squeezes my hands, pulling my arms more tightly around her. "What you and I are doing. Afraid I'd fall so hard for another soul, I could never survive losing him..."

"It scares me, too," I whisper, kissing her tear-streaked cheek.

"But it's too late now."

My heart stops at the sound of her words, and my throat tightens. "Good, because I can never let you go." She sighs, satisfied, melting into me some more. I nuzzle her neck, savoring this intimate moment and thanking God for giving this grumpy, old cowboy a second chance.

Finally, I add, "But that pain and heartache is also what makes you such an understanding and gifted writer, especially when it comes to grief, loss, and yearning."

"Wait, did you read one of my books?"

"Last night...*Love's Promise*. It was beautiful, Chanel, and your words...I don't know how to describe them. They healed my heart...in ways I'm still trying to comprehend. They let me know it was okay to want happiness again...to want it with you."

She lets out another sob, wetting the bare skin on my wrist with her tears. "My experiences in life are reflected in my books, along with my greatest hopes and wildest beliefs. Like my belief in a love so strong it'll see two people through any storm life throws their way, and my desire for a place where I belong, with the family I never had but always desperately yearned for."

Her words wrap around my heart. "I couldn't have described the motivation behind my book any better than you just did."

She pauses for a moment. "I can see that in your work. By the way, I should have said this sooner, but I was still off-kilter because of the whole mistaken identity thing. *Sublime Incantations* is what made me believe in love again. It saved my heart and my career, and it put me on a circuitous course to meeting you. I can't describe how much your words and art mean to me. How much you mean to me."

Sobs wrack her frame. "I don't want to be an ice princess anymore, holding people I care about at arm's length for fear of losing them. I want warmth and happiness, love and family, and I want it with you...and Maddie, Eldon, Véronique, and Avery...even if it means risking my heart."

Turning her in my arms to face me, my eyes dance over her tear-streaked face, etching this moment on my heart. Chuckling, I say, "As much as I appreciate the inclusiveness of your love declaration, how about we keep it about you and me for right now?"

"That *was* a love declaration, wasn't it?" she says breathlessly, awed by her own words.

"And so is this." Without hesitation, I pocket my gloves, cupping her impossibly soft cheek in my rough hand. Slowly traveling the distance between us, I'm aware of everything about this moment. How her pretty pink lips part in a smile. The way her eyelids flutter and close when my lips brush against hers. And her delicious smell enveloping me.

My hand slides from her cheek to her neck, leaving goosebumps where my fingers blaze trails of fire on her flesh, coming to rest at the nape of her neck and the inviting sweep of her décolletage. Savoring the feel of her petal-soft mouth on mine, I deepen the kiss, my heart racing and wanting so much more with this beautiful woman.

Her tiny hands stroke my beard and find their way into my wavy hair, and when she pulls back breathlessly, her eyes sparkle with love. Palming my cheeks, her thumbs rest on my dimples, and she flirts, "I thought we needed to be under the mistletoe for this, Mr. Heart."

I chuckle, wrapping my arms more tightly around her waist. "I think we just proved we can manage without. Don't you? Otherwise, I'll cover every square inch of the ranch in that silly green plant."

"The owl and mice will like it," she teases, a slight strain to her voice.

"I promise, Eldon and I will get that sorted out today, Goldie. After all, you strike me as the kind of girl who prefers rustic to roughing it."

"Swooping owls and skittering mice may be my limit."

"Noted." I steal another taste of her sugar-sweet mouth, my soul happily crashing into hers...finding my respite and my home. I don't know how long we spend like this, reveling in each other's tenderest touches and whispered sentiments, but I can't keep the sunshiny blonde to myself forever. Not on Christmas Day.

Finally, begrudgingly, I ask, stroking her silky golden locks. "Are you ready to celebrate Christmas with our family?"

She nods, palming my cheeks, her eyes swimming with joy. "Being here with you like this, Chase, feeling like I belong and am loved and needed is the best gift of all. Thank you for giving me my heart's desire."

If you loved Chase & Chanel's story in *Mistletoe Mismatch*, then you'll love Kris & Meri's story in *Mistletoe Magic*.

CHECK IT OUT HERE

Find all the books in the Mistletoe Kisses series at:

MISTLETOE KISSES FULL SERIES

ABOUT THE AUTHOR

E.B. Silva writes sweet, clean contemporary romances with all the feels. Her stories feature gruff cowboys and mountain men and the sassy, quirky woman they fall head over heels for.

Favorite tropes include grumpy/sunshine, fake engagement, marriage of convenience, found family, and best friends to lovers.

If you like cozy small-town vibes, expansive mountain views, and lovable characters who always find happily ever afters with their soulmates, E.B. Silva's your girl. Satisfying, heartfelt HEAs guaranteed!

Head to E.B. Silva's website to never miss out on upcoming and new releases as well as freebies and deals: www.ebsilva.com.

instagram.com/authorebsilva

tiktok.com/@authorebsilva

facebook.com/authorebsilva